DEAD RECKONING

MICHAEL CORBIN RAY
& THERESE VANNIER

DEAD
RECKONING

BAAA! PRESS

Published by Baaa! Press
www.baaapress.com

This book is a work of fiction based on true events.
All characters, real and imagined, are long dead.
We've stayed with the truth as far as we can know it.
We've taken liberties and guesses with the rest.

ISBN 978-1-940776-09-5

For twenty-three men

of the Delphy and the Young,

and for all who risk their lives in service at sea.

Full fathom five thy father lies,
  Of his bones are coral made:
Those are pearls that were his eyes:
  Nothing of him that doth fade,
But doth suffer a sea-change
Into something rich and strange.

—W.S.

Dead Reckoning

HALFWAY THROUGH THE OCEAN CROSSING, SEVEN DAYS after leaving Yokohama, the ss *President Cleveland* became in an instant a ghost ship. The news arrived via wireless. As the liner carved its straight steady route north of gray Hawaiian waters, a radio operator listened intently, jotted a few notes on a sheet of paper, and handed this paper to the ship's captain. The message, intended to warn of potentially difficult seas due to seismic activity in the western Pacific, did not spare the details of disaster. Word of the Great Kantō Earthquake of 1923 spread from captain to crew and from crew to passengers: Tokyo and Yokohama had fallen, along with much of Chiba, Kanagawa, and Shizuoka; typhoon winds whipped firestorms through the rubble; wave after tsunami wave rose up to attack the broken land. It was too soon to count the dead, which in the end would number more than 100,000 souls.

The tragedy shocked the American businessmen and missionaries on board. In recent days they had grown fond of Japan's exotic customs and people. They gathered in the ship's lounge to recall the temples and bright pagodas, the geishas and the gardens, and wondered aloud what still stood. They reminisced about acquaintances left behind and prayed for their survival or, failing that, their salvation. For the ship's many Japanese guests, however, the news simply ripped their hearts from their chests. Beloved friends, wives, husbands, mothers, brothers, sisters, fathers, sons and daughters and nephews and nieces, fates unknown and unknowable, haunted every thought, every movement, every breath. They stood at the stern and looked out past the wake, past the horizon, past the setting sun, and they cried for their loss.

Eugene Dooman heard the news while taking breakfast in the first class dining room. The buzz among the passengers had been building all morning, but he had shut it out in favor of a book given to him by a compatriot before the voyage, an account of events leading to the Great War which he found so far to be mediocre and rather an apologia for certain diplomatic missteps.

"I say, Mr. Dooman? Have you heard? It's terribly horrific."

The woman, plump and overdressed, was the wife of an industrialist. Railroad people. Weeks earlier Dooman had guided her husband through a series of embassy parties, introducing him to his Japanese counterparts, translating as needed, and wishing them success in their joint endeavors. Now she was practically bursting with gossip, her girdle tight enough already as it was.

He thanked her politely for the information, diplomatically even, and at the next opportunity made his way forward to the ship's bridge and the radio room, where he requested a message be relayed on his behalf to the U.S. State Department:

> Please advise upon arrival San Francisco should
> Eugene H. Dooman, secretary at American Embassy
> Tokyo, return to Japan on first available ship?

Then he went to his cabin to rest. He was thirty-three years old and tired. It had been an eventful year. The decision to leave Tokyo, initially nothing but a well-earned relaxation from service, now took on the added significance of being the third time in nine months that he had narrowly escaped death.

The first occasion had been an ill-fated winter voyage to Vladivostok. Sent to assess the situation in that Russian backwater after its fall to the Communists,

Dooman's ship had met an unexpected storm hours after setting out. Ice on the foredeck had accumulated so heavily that it weighed the bow down into the water, raising the stern and propellers and making navigation and forward movement impossible. It seemed all that kept them from foundering was the buoyancy of the ice itself, but there would be no guarantees if the ship turned on its side and took water. The crew spent days and nights in a losing battle of hammering and chipping and shaving at the frozen mass until at last the storm broke and they limped into port a week late, the authorities having already given them up as lost. Several months later, on a brief hiking holiday in the Japanese Alps, Dooman had taken a misstep—upon which carelessness he preferred not to dwell—that led to a tumble down a mountainside, his fall arrested just feet from ruin by the fortunate placement of a single protruding boulder. And now this latest trouble. He pictured his Tokyo apartment destroyed and in flames, his books and bed buried and burning, and thanked God for once again sparing him by the slightest of margins.

He was not a superstitious man—he would never make the claim that these things came only in threes—but surely after all he had been through the odds should be in his favor for a while.

That afternoon he tried to mingle with his fellow passengers but found their worries dull, self-serving, and ignorant of the Japan he knew so well. Born in Osaka to missionary parents who had emigrated from the turbulence of their native Iran, Dooman's fierce and firm loyalty to the United States came weighted with a worldly experience. As a child he spoke Japanese fluently, perhaps even better than his English. He had spent plenty of time stateside at boarding school and university, but after graduation his employment with the diplomatic service sent him straight back to Tokyo—which, he could not forget, now lay in ruins.

He would be needed there. He wished he had never left.

Dooman visited the Japanese passengers but they were too broken by the news. Unlike him, they had left loved ones behind. He was unmarried, his parents long since retired and living in America, and the fate of missing co-workers carried less weight than that of missing wives and children. He checked in daily with the ship's officers and the radio room, but he received no instruction from his superiors and the ship sailed on with no sign of the feared difficult seas.

And so at the end of an otherwise uneventful fourteen-day voyage, on the morning of September 7, 1923, the *Cleveland* motored into San Francisco Bay and unloaded at Angel Island for the dual filters of customs and immigration. Dooman's status with the State Department expedited his clearance but to no great advantage. Instead of waiting in line with the others, he waited outside at the dock by the empty ferry as one by one his fellow passengers rejoined him. For the most part, among the Americans at least, their mourning for Japan had given way to excitement at reaching their destination. They were eager to get on with it and annoyed by the slow pace of processing the Japanese and Chinese arrivals, a good number of whom were pulled aside for further questioning and an extended stay in the island's detention center.

At last the ferry left the dock and headed across the bay. As many as could fit, Dooman among them, clung to the rail at the wide bow to watch the city come into focus. Consolation of sorts could be found in the bustling wharf ahead and the busy profile of buildings carpeting the hillsides. Factories, banks, hotels, residences—less than a score of years had passed since earthquake and fire had leveled this great city as well. Tokyo, like San Francisco, would rise again.

Fishing boats, freighters, and Navy warships studded the water and filled the docks ahead. Several dozen of the latter lay at rest, identical sleek gray knives lined side by side like a trick done with mirrors, their heavy gun turrets locked forward and aft in proud repose. The ferry passed almost in the shadow of one anchored destroyer before turning for the wharf, where workers called out as they guided crates from ships to dock and from dock to ship. Nets of tired fish rose slowly from their holds, draining water in scale-glittered rainbows.

The ferry's crew tied up and the gates wheeled open. After a moment of hesitation the passengers understood they were free to depart. Dooman nearly lost his grip on his luggage amidst the bumping and pushing as everyone unloaded and dispersed in a rush. Soon it was hard to distinguish his fellow travelers from ordinary San Franciscans, except for the confused looks on those trying to orient themselves to the new city. He supposed he was one of those. He set down his bag and mentally noted the compass points, having studied a map before disembarking the liner. An electric streetcar and several jitney cabs were possibilities. Walking to his hotel would be a bit much.

He was about to take another step forward when an excitement of Navy sailors surged past, immobilizing mere civilians with their loud momentum and enthusiasm for liberty. They were young and low-ranking and boisterous, and their quest for fun or trouble or maybe both had led them here. It was ten o'clock in the morning and the height of Prohibition, but Dooman could smell the rum at five paces.

"Step right up, gentlemen, test your wits." A young man unfolded a small portable table and dropped a satchel beneath it. "Find the lucky lady and the money is yours."

"No thanks, kid," said a passing sailor. "I know your game."

And the game was simple: three playing cards face down on the table, rapidly shuffled by expert hands, turned up to reveal two black jacks and a queen of diamonds. Dooman had seen this sport before but he admired the man's skill as two more sailors approached the table.

"I'll give it a go," said one, dropping a ten dollar bill onto a card.

"Hey diddle diddle," said the dealer, turning the card face up, "the queen's in the middle." He paid twenty dollars to the lucky sailor, who cheered and shook hands with his companion.

"All right, another round. I have three cards in my hand. Two jacks and a queen. I shuffle them up and mix their places, and if you tell me where she is, you'll have happy faces."

The second sailor borrowed money from his friend and laid it on a card. The dealer turned it over and shook his head, not very well hiding his disappointment.

"Bad luck for me, gentlemen. I do believe you hope to clean me out. But I don't cry when I lose and I won't sing when I win." He paid the second sailor then he worked his fingers a bit, shaking off the loss and readying himself to try again. He picked up his showy patter. "The red queen is the one you're after. Ten will get you twenty and twenty gets you forty. I have two chances to your one but if your eye is faster than my hand you win every time. Find the lady and triple your money."

A new man, drawn by the easy pickings, joined the game with his own ten dollars. This time, though, luck favored the dealer, whose hands pocketed the bill so quickly that the man had no chance to object.

"She's a cruel mistress. She teases and tarts. But I'm a fair host and you'll always have another chance. Remember, it's two cards to me and one to you. Follow with your eye while I shuffle the three. Here she is, and here, and here, now what do you see?"

The novice gambler hesitated, studying the backs of the cards. Where was the trick?

"This is a game for players, not watchers," said the dealer. "Who's brave enough to take a chance?"

The first sailor threw down another ten dollars. Again he had the winner.

"And that's how it's done. Nice work from the man with the sharp eye, a servant of his country no less, and surely a better man than I am. Find the honey and win the money. It's your lucky day. Jack, jack, and queen, and she's the one you want."

So this was America at last. There was nothing Dooman could do for the people of Tokyo, not now, not from here. He let himself relax for the first time in a week, realizing all at once how difficult he had been making this on himself. There was no point in dwelling on problems with no solutions, not when you were a free man in a land of opportunity. These sailors, this street gambler, they would never burden their lives with such intractable thoughts. They simply lived. They lived impulsively and well, never questioning their own worth. It seemed easy enough. Dooman thought he would join them.

He removed his wallet from a jacket pocket. It bulged with his traveling cash. From the stack he pulled a twenty dollar bill and placed it on a card.

"Why not?" he said. "Let's make this an auspicious start to my American furlough."

It came as something of a surprise, then, when the man turned the card to reveal one of the jacks and in the same smooth motion removed Dooman's money from the table. How—

"And when the dough goes down, the lady can't be found. Let me explain the game, friend. I have three cards. Two belong to me but the queen is yours. I take no bets from paupers, cripples, or orphan children, for this red lady is no kind mother. She runs, she hides, but catch her and you're in the money. Ten will get you back the twenty you lost."

Dooman tracked the man's hands as he spoke. The play was straightforward. The queen was turned face down in the middle then moved to the left, to the right, then back to the left. Dooman bet again and again he lost.

"It seems you've still got your sea legs, sir, and the salt spray stings your vision."

"I'm fourteen days by ship out of Tokyo," Dooman said. "But I'd say the difficulty lies less in my eyes than your hands. You're very skilled with those cards."

"It passes the time," the man said. "It keeps me out of trouble." He gave Dooman a wink, riffled the cards once more, and spread them face up on the table. There wasn't a jack or queen among them, just the four of clubs repeated three times like the sails of a ship. "How's that for a boat?"

Astonished, Dooman stared at the cards, playing the man's quick, short hand movements back in his mind. "How—"

But at that moment a sharp whistle sounded nearby in the crowd. A uniformed sailor blew a loud warning with two of his fingers in his mouth as two police officers closed fast on the game. The man with the cards reacted instantly, grabbing his satchel from the ground and knocking over the table. The cards scattered. The man ran.

Before Dooman had the chance to comprehend the situation, the whistling sailor was on him.

"Go, sir!" the man shouted. "Gambling is a serious crime in this city. Don't let them catch you."

The sailor grabbed Dooman by the shoulders, turned him around, and gave him a push to get him started. It seemed an overreaction. Surely the police would be inclined to ignore such a minor offense, especially from a respectable, honest man who came out on the losing end of the game. But again the sailor's hands were on him, turning him around once more, and again he spoke in a voice much louder than necessary.

"Wait, sir. Don't forget."

Dooman felt the man guiding his arm to his luggage, helping his hand grip the handle, helping him lift the heavy case, then turning him back and forcing him on his way.

"Fly, sir. Fly now. I'll misdirect the police for you."

Confused and even a bit ashamed, Dooman took a few steps into the crowd before pausing and collecting his wits. He turned back, prepared at last to speak, but the man was nowhere to be seen. The other two sailors, though, the two who had been so good at the game, now blocked the way of the hurried policemen.

"Officers," said the first man, "I'd like to file a complaint. That thief stole my hard-earned wages."

"It was a fixed game," said the other. "Nothing fair about it."

The policemen attempted to move past the two sailors, their eyes fixed on the fleeing cardsman as he escaped the crowded walkway and crossed into the busy street beyond.

"A complaint, sir. I demand you take my statement."

"Move aside," one of the officers replied. He shoved the sailor away and continued his pursuit.

"I see him running," the second sailor said. "There he is." But the direction the sailor pointed was opposite the direction in which the gambler had run. The second officer batted the man's pointing hand before rejoining the chase.

It was then that worldly wise Eugene Dooman, secretary at the United States Embassy in Tokyo, newly arrived upon the shores of his own strange country, realized the way in which he had been fleeced.

FRIDAY

Emmett Haines adjusted the strap of his satchel. There was nothing heavy in there to slow him down, just a few essentials that might come in handy. It could have been a metaphor for his life up to this point. Two policemen followed perhaps twenty seconds behind. He ran faster than those well-fed lawmen but the geographical advantage was theirs. They knew the ins and outs of these unfamiliar streets and their whistles would soon alert reinforcements. Somewhere in there was the second half of the metaphor.

Haines veered left into dense automobile traffic, where through the noise of horns and engines he heard his pursuers curse and yell. "Stop! Halt!" one of the policemen called out at him. And then one to the other: "That way!"

Haines dodged around the front of a trolley then bent low as he ran, ducking out of sight. On the far sidewalk he slalomed past fruit carts and newsstands, passed under a ladder, hurdled a stray dog, pardoned himself to slow-moving pedestrians, and disappeared around the next corner.

This was San Francisco's Barbary Coast, famed for sin and depravity from its earliest days. He had heard the stories even as a young boy in landlocked Missouri, raucous tales raucously told by uncles with the itch for adventure. A crackdown on gamblers and other purveyors of vice in recent years had put a cap on much of the fun, but aficionados of the degenerate arts could still find their pleasures. A man had to work harder now to get around the law, but the law could always be gotten around.

Haines enjoyed the game. He played less for the money than for the pleasure of performing a hard-earned skill. He felt sharper with a deck of cards in his hands, chatting up some money-blind stranger, than he ever did following dull, repetitive orders in the hold of a ship.

He scanned the street ahead, a long, straight run with few opportunities for hiding. But here, right here beside him, he found a place. He reached into the pockets of his trousers and sifted through a handful of change, retrieved two coins, and purchased a ticket at a kiosk. He hurried through twin doors, taking deep breaths to calm his heartbeat and ease the sweat of the chase. Trying not to draw attention, he slowed his pace as he crossed the lobby and entered the theater. His eyes adjusted to a darkness lit only by the filmstrip projected on screen. It was a comic story of some sort with a man faking illness to catch an ambulance ride across town in order to get to work on time. The work didn't seem worth getting to.

The auditorium was only a quarter full. Haines walked down the aisle to an empty row and took a seat toward the middle. It was hot in the theater, or maybe it was just him. Still, he reached into his satchel and took out a U.S. Navy uniform shirt, which he pulled over his head, over the shirt he was already wearing. He then put on a sailor's cap and slouched low in his seat. In a familiar twist, the man in the film was now on the run from the cops, a scene that involved more acrobatic climbing of buildings than Haines was accustomed to.

He felt something hit the back of his neck—a quick tap, a light scratch that tumbled away. He brushed it off, figuring it for a moth or other insect. But moths don't say *psshhht* and they don't throw popcorn. A piece grazed his cheek.

"What the hell—" he started. But as he turned to confront his tormentor the doors at the rear of the theater opened and the two policemen stepped inside. Haines turned back to the screen and sank even lower into his seat. The sweat on his brow seeped beneath the band of his cap.

He sensed the two men as they made their way forward, tapping the aisle armrests with their billy clubs as they passed. Their eyes could not have adjusted to the darkness just yet. Haines considered his options. If he were going to run he should do it as the police approached the front of the theater, before they turned to face the audience again. That would give him a modest head start. But then without warning a woman three seats back stood and moved forward, entering his row, blocking his path, and sat beside him.

"I know you," she whispered.

"I'm sure you don't."

This was the popcorn thrower. She wore her hair in a short bob, right in line with other forward thinking ladies of the day. She was fashionably if a bit provocatively dressed, with fringes and hems in all the right places and lipstick that caught the flicker of light from the moving picture on screen. It was too dark to make her out fully but he was sure she was attractive and he was sure he had never seen her before in his life. He would have remembered.

"I've seen your game," she said. "You and your friends. I've seen you around. Do you think she's pretty?"

"What?"

The two policemen had reached the front of the theater. They peered back at the audience, squinting at the dark faces. One or two in the crowd turned their way as well, annoyed by the whispers.

"Mildred Davis," the woman said, ignoring the looks.

"Who?"

"The girl. In the movie. The actress. Do you think she's pretty?"

Shush, came the scolds from the dark. The policemen began to move up the aisle.

"Sure," Haines said. "Why not."

"I think so too. They're married in real life, you know. But he was with Bebe Daniels before."

Would this woman not shut up? As the two policemen drew nearer she held out her box of Cracker Jack, offering him a taste. He declined.

"Do you think she's prettier than me? You can be honest. I don't mind."

"How would I know?" Haines said, exasperated. He gave up trying to hide. "No, right, you're prettier. But I'm sure she has a better personality."

And then a curious thing—the woman set aside her Cracker Jack and leaned over to kiss Haines long and deep. A flashlight beam lit them up. They turned, blinking into the light, barely able to make out the outline of a policeman standing behind it. For a moment Haines wondered what the interruption could be about, and how the timing could be any worse.

"You two," the man said, "save it for later. There's decent people here don't need to witness your lasciviousness."

And with that the officer and his partner left the theater, their suspect nowhere to be found.

Haines stared at the woman, more than a little stunned.

"You're welcome," she said, and she settled into her seat to watch the rest of the movie in silence.

)O)O(

The St. Francis Hotel, normally the epitome of elegance and sophistication, had a problem with a guest. While finely dressed civilians milled about the lobby, several uniformed Navy captains and a number of lieutenants among them, one gentleman at wit's end harassed the head clerk at the reception desk.

"As I told you, I have a reservation," the man said. "The reservation is not the problem."

"What can I do to help you, sir? A reservation doesn't do either of us any good if you don't have the money to pay for it."

"That's not—I have money. But I don't have my billfold. It's been stolen. By common thieves and sailors."

The clerk made his best attempt at a sympathetic frown but business was business. "So you have no money?"

"Correct. But no. I only need to get it back."

"Problem solved, then," the clerk replied, smiling again. "See us when you've recovered your property and we'll gladly get you settled."

The man's frustration only increased. They had been at this a while and progress seemed elusive.

"Wait. No. What I need—I need to check in first, then I can contact the State Department. They'll have an advance for me. I've been two weeks at sea, sir, and I need an honest bed."

His voice cracked as he spoke. He was not used to this. He considered himself a problem solver. Such direct confrontation was alien to his diplomatic nature. Not only that, but his embarrassing dilemma had begun to draw attention from the hotel's more refined guests. In a mirror on the wall before him he caught a glimpse of an imposing figure, a uniformed military officer, strong and authoritative, approaching from behind. He feared he was about to be escorted from the premises.

"Is this man causing trouble?" The query to the clerk came from a deep bass voice, one accustomed to command.

Dooman—for it was Eugene Dooman after all, only this morning arrived from Japan and robbed of his bankroll—turned to face his fate.

"My stars. Ed?"

Dooman was shocked to recognize the captain, who cracked a friendly, mischievous smile. This was good news at last indeed.

"How are you, Eugene? What's it been, two years?"

"I arrived just this morning. I've had a terrible time of it." He did not mean to let loose his complaint with such weak emotion but it could not be helped.

"Captain Watson, you'll vouch for Mr. Dooman?" The clerk was happy enough to pass the burden along.

"Vouch for him? Hell, when I served as Naval Attache in Japan, Gene here saved my bacon more than once. He's a good man to know if you're navigating the political waters of the Far East."

"But I'm afraid I'm entirely out of my depth back home in America." There was the self-pity again. He would have to check himself soon. "I feel like such a noodle."

"Tell me your troubles."

And so Dooman let it all out in a rush: "I've been robbed, Ed. All my cash, my identification, my letter of credit, my ticket to Los Angeles. I'm in quite the pickle. And I hate to say it but the culprits are some of your very own sailors." He avoided mention of the card game. He was too embarrassed to admit he had been taken by such a folly. In fact it was only upon reaching the hotel that he had even discovered his greater loss, and so it could have happened anywhere along the route—but no, he knew in his heart the men who had picked his pocket. He was sure of it.

The story cast the briefest shadow across the captain's visage but the powerful man kept it cool and light for the sake of his distraught friend.

"Well then it's great luck you ran into a comrade who owes you a favor, isn't it? Let's see about getting you some harsh justice against those hooligans."

The captain then clapped Dooman upon the back, settled his account with the clerk, and retired to the hotel's lounge to catch up on old times with his old friend.

XOXOX

Emmett Haines stepped lightly through the door of the cafe. It almost felt as if he were floating. But then he saw his three friends seated at a table near the back. That grounded him. He tapped across the linoleum and took the open seat next to Jack Pearson and directly across from Earl Grady, who was still slowly finishing his lunch. Knowing Grady, this was probably his second lunch anyway. Pearson and Henry Forsythe had already pushed their empty plates to the side.

"Look who's too good to eat with his crew," Pearson said. Pearson was by far the strongest and the tallest of the four, although he bore the curse of being defined in the eyes of strangers not by his strength but by the bottle-bottom-thick glasses that made his eyes appear the wrong size for his head.

The three men still wore their Navy uniforms from their encounter that morning, while Haines had returned his sailor's cap and shirt to his satchel.

"I had a close call," he said. "I had to hide out."

"Our boy's in love," Grady noted, coming up for air from his egg salad sandwich. "I can see it in his eyes."

"I can smell it on his shirt," said Forsythe.

Haines ignored the digs. He pushed Grady's lunch plate closer to Grady, clearing some space on the table. He took out a deck of cards and tapped them like a pack of cigarettes. He smoothed out the tablecloth, brushing away crumbs.

"So what happened?" Pearson asked. Pearson had been the lookout that morning, blowing the whistle at the first sign of police. Forsythe and Grady, the other two sidemen in the game, had played the roles of lucky winners.

Haines fanned and flipped the cards and began to practice his flourishes: springs and waterfalls and charlier cuts, the cards flying from hand to hand with ease. "The usual," he said. "Got chased. Got away." He kept it nonchalant. Jack Pearson could be unpredictable. He was a man of moods, most of them morose, suspicious, and—when it came to Haines—even a bit jealous. Haines spread the cards across the table once more, flipped them to show a mixed deck, then flipped them back and brought them into a stack. "Come on, everybody in. Time to settle up."

Haines pulled a small roll of mixed ten and twenty dollar bills from his pocket and placed it in the center of the table. Forsythe added a few bills of his own and Haines went back to shuffling the deck. One, two, three times he shuffled, then he fanned and flipped again. Now the cards were perfectly ordered by suit as if they were a fresh deck. Forsythe and Pearson ignored the trick but Grady watched, mesmerized, sandwich hanging halfway to his open mouth.

"Earl, spill."

Forsythe nudged Grady to break the spell. Grady took one hand off his sandwich to fish money from his pocket.

"Nothing to add, Jack?" Haines asked. "Okay, you divvy. Eighty to me and forty was Henry's for capital.

The rest is profit four ways. I reckon we're up fifty each after last night and this morning."

As Pearson gathered and counted the money, Haines went back to his practice shuffles and flourishes.

"So who's the girl this time, Em?" Grady shoved the last of his sandwich into his mouth. Still chewing, he wiped his hands on his uniform pants and put his attention on the cards.

"Another port, another port," said Forsythe.

"No, this one, she's different. She's interesting."

"Interesting? You really are in love."

Pearson scowled at that. Haines held out the deck and spread the cards for Grady. Grady knew the rules. He took a card and peeked at its face—the four of clubs— then he returned it to the stack. He watched as Haines shuffled.

"She's smart and she knows the score," Haines said. He spread the deck face up across the table, gesturing for Grady to find his card.

"Fifty it is." Pearson finished the cash count and distributed the profits. "If she knows the score," he gruffed, "she knows she won't see you again."

"She'll see me."

"We gotta be back to the *Delphy* by midnight. Captain Watson will tan your hide if you miss another roll call."

Grady, meanwhile, had given up searching the deck. "I don't see it, Em. Where's my card?"

"Her name's Ruby. We're just looking to have a little fun." Haines reached across the table and tapped the salt shaker. Grady picked it up and turned it around, studying it. "I'm meeting her in an hour."

"I don't like her already," Pearson said. "Are you running her or is she running you?"

Grady began to unscrew the lid of the salt shaker, carefully at first then pushing harder through the grind of salt in the threads.

"She helped me out. I figured I'd cut her in on a little score."

The lid came undone and slipped from Grady's hand, spilling salt across the table.

"Christ, Earl," Forsythe exclaimed. "Keep it together."

But Grady, unconcerned by the bad luck, stuck his finger into the shaker and pulled out a folded playing card: his missing four of clubs. He looked at Haines with wonder.

"How?"

But Haines continued his face-off against Pearson, who accused him of taking a risk.

"I can handle myself," Haines said. "She might have a line on that dupe from the ferry this morning. Did you all get eyes on that fat stack in his wallet? That's worth another try."

If Pearson gave the most minor flinch at that, the most minor tell, nobody remarked on it. Grady, for one, remained especially oblivious.

"Did you see this?" he asked, waving the bent card at his friends. "How did he do that?"

"Same way he did it last time, Earl, and the time before that." Forsythe was patient with Grady but more concerned with the tension across the table.

"But I picked the card. How does he know?"

"You pick the same damn card every time," Pearson snapped. "You ain't figured it out yet? It's like his signature. You don't think maybe you're picking the card he wants you to pick?"

"Well, yeah, but … but I'm the one who picked it."

"My God. Earl. Think."

Grady looked from Haines to the magical four of clubs and back to Haines again, still puzzled. Haines took the break as his cue to stand. He pocketed his share of the cash.

"I don't like it, Emmett," Pearson said. "You can't quit your crew like this."

"Who's quitting? I've got a day off and a nice girl to spend it with. If we pick up the game with this guy, don't worry, I'll cut you fellas in on the take."

"You sure, Emmett? You don't want backup?"

"I already have a mother. I don't need four. You fellas enjoy liberty tonight. Try to have a good time for once, Jack."

Haines waved goodbye as he left. Pearson watched him disappear from view. Then he looked back at the chaos on the table, at the spray of spilled salt and the ruined playing card and Grady's mess of a second lunch.

"Goddammit, Earl."

"What did I do?"

Pearson wiped the salt back at Grady, pushing a good portion off the table and onto his friend's lap.

"I got a bad feeling he's not coming back," he said.

※※※

Ruby and Emmett had arranged to meet in the park across the street from the St. Francis Hotel. On her way to her apartment to freshen up before the date she stopped at a shop on Market Street to buy ingredients for a picnic lunch. She bought bread and jam and cold roast beef.

The kiss had been an impulsive move. She wasn't sure why she had done it, but she had a feeling about this man. Her feelings had gotten her into trouble before, but then again she was right as often as not.

She arrived at the rendezvous point first and as she waited she began to worry that he wouldn't show. But of course he would show, she told herself. She had a feeling. What had she been thinking, roast beef and jam? What kind of lunch was that? And then there he was.

Their second meeting was more awkward than the first. He didn't kiss her cheek or even her hand or make any move to touch her at all, although he did offer to carry the basket.

They strolled through the park to a bench and sat facing the entrance to the hotel. They talked about the weather. She asked how long he would be in the city. He came from a small town near a big river; he had been a sailor for less than a year and was stationed in San Diego. She truly had admired his card game from afar, having seen him and his friends run their monte play several times in the past few days. He had learned the trade from his uncles, he told her. She warned him away from certain neighborhoods and told him the best times of day to avoid the local police patrols. This was the business, but it was more than that.

"This is quite an afternoon you've arranged, Mr. Haines," Ruby said. "Makes a girl feel special."

"Your other fellas don't take you out scouting for marks?"

"Never on the first date. I'm not that kind of girl."

He laughed, always a good sign.

"I hope you'll forgive my presumption, then. I don't have long before my ship sails so I figured we'd skip ahead to the good stuff." He nodded toward a man stepping up to the hotel entrance. "What about him?"

She gave the man an appraising glance. That was all she needed.

"Look at his shoes," she said.

"Right. And the worn cuffs."

"There's no money there and I'd feel bad taking it if there was. How about that one?"

She was testing Haines as much as he was testing her. He looked to this next man leaving the hotel, well dressed, confident, and strong.

"Sure, but those knuckles," he said.

"He's a fighter?"

"He likes to fight, at least. There's easier ways to make a buck."

A car stopped in front of the hotel and with unneeded assistance from both the driver and the hotel's doorman, an expensive looking woman in a red dress exited the car and entered the building.

"And that one," Haines said, "she'd read me in a heartbeat."

"I know her. She would."

He didn't ask, but Ruby could tell he was curious.

"It's a small town if you live here," she said. "It doesn't take long to find your place."

They each ate a few bites of their lunch until Ruby found a way to begin again, pointing her sandwich at the hotel. "This is where they took down Fatty Arbuckle, you know. Talk about a party where everyone was working an angle."

"You were there?"

"Friends of friends. Just gossip. They say now he didn't do it, but there wasn't nobody in that room who wasn't guilty of something."

"Aren't we all?"

"A girl's gotta do what a girl's gotta do."

Another man exited the hotel and this one caught her eye. He wore a well tailored suit with everything in its right place but there was something of an insecurity about him, a forced confidence masking doubt—she had a feeling.

"What about that one?" she asked.

Haines looked at the man and lit up. "That's him. That's our guy."

He started to stand, started to wave, was close to making eye contact with Eugene Dooman across the street, when a Navy captain emerged from the building and clasped the man's shoulder with a friendly hand.

"Damn," Haines said. Then he turned and dove in on Ruby, taking the favor of another kiss. She didn't mind as this kiss went on for longer than the one she had given him. After a while he came up for air and apologized. "How was I to know the man's a friend of my captain?"

With the palm of her hand against his chest she felt his heart racing. Was it from the close call or something else? She felt her own heart racing as well. They kissed again as the two men across the street climbed into a cab and drove away. She closed her eyes. She had a feeling about this Emmett Haines and she wanted to hold onto it—to hold onto him.

At last he pulled back to look at her. He looked at her eyes for a long time, for the first time, and she knew it wouldn't be the last.

She had a feeling.

XXX

Earl Grady and Henry Forsythe spent the day in half-hearted search of their friend. With no expectation of finding him in the unfamiliar city they stopped by the few places they had all discovered together—a cafe on the wharf, a secret Chinese gambling hall, a peep show—while Pearson went ahead to an underground speakeasy that had served as their rendezvous for the past two nights. He planned to be drunk by the time they arrived. He was.

As Grady and Forsythe approached the unmarked door in the narrow alley they heard music from the other side. A bare bulb above the door cast circles of red light on the alley walls.

"Red sky at night," said Grady.

"Red eyes in the morning," replied his friend.

They knocked and a sliding panel opened in the center of the door. A pair of rugged eyes stared out at them. Then the door opened and they stepped inside. They parted a heavy velvet curtain into a main room already crowded with sailors and fashionable civilians. They found Pearson alone at a table with a glass of melting ice in his hand, an empty bottle beside it.

"I hoped he'd be here," he said. "He's not here."

"You think he's in trouble?"

Grady and Forsythe pulled out a pair of chairs and sat, leaving one empty spot at the table.

"Sure he's in trouble."

Pearson tilted his empty drink to the light. He squinted at it through his glasses as if trying to conjure a refill from the smoke-choked air.

"Em wouldn't quit like that. I don't believe it."

"I saw it in his eyes. You saw it too."

Forsythe wasn't convinced, not yet. He would need a few drinks to catch up with Pearson's way of thinking. "I saw he was crazy over some skirt but a sailor gets over that when the bell rings."

The party continued around them, oblivious to their glum mood. People drank and smoked and danced.

They rolled their dice and came up winners and losers. The house took its cut. Pearson tried and failed to wave down a waiter.

"If he's quitting we gotta stop him," Grady said. "He'll be throwing his life away. What's he gonna do without the Navy?"

This was followed by salty words about the state of things—about how the grunts at the bottom of any organization were always first to bear the hardship from decisions made far above their pay grade. It was Congress who cut the Navy's budget, it was admirals who prized machines above men, battleships above destroyers, and now it was the poor sailors sweating double and triple shifts below deck to make up for it. The entire fleet had been running understaffed for years and it was no surprise that a man working one hundred hours a week, week after week, might not be a happy man.

"But to tell the truth, Earl," Forsythe said, "out of the four of us, Em's the one needs the Navy least of all. We need him more than he needs us."

That was enough for Pearson. He slammed his glass to the table, losing what remained of his ice.

"Bullshit. A team's a team. Every cog in a machine has a job. If one cog quits he lets down his fellow cogs. When you take an oath you keep it."

The alcohol was giving him trouble with his words but at the same time giving him more words to say. He stared at his empty glass for a moment then reached into his pocket and pulled out a handful of crumpled bills. He shoved the money at Grady.

"Get another bottle," Pearson said, "and three more glasses. Em's not here, we're going to have to drink his share until he shows. That's what being a team's about."

✕✕✕✕

Eugene Dooman remained unsettled by his ordeal, although a hot meal from something other than a ship's galley went a long way toward reviving his mood.

Captain Watson had insisted that Dooman order the lamb and had then requested broiled mackerel for himself. They added boiled potatoes, stewed celery in cream, mixed melon supreme, a vanilla pudding soufflé, and— Prohibition be damned—two bottles of French wine, which Watson assured him were quite good.

Captain Watson had been a great boon to Dooman's day but his enthusiasm for finding the culprits and Dooman's wallet had waned. There were two full Navy squadrons in port, over thirty ships with a hundred men on each. Searching every crew for a wallet that had likely been rifled and tossed seemed a quixotic quest, the captain had argued.

They had taken a stroll along the waterfront that afternoon, but within only a few blocks decided it best to return to the St. Francis and enjoy lunch instead. Now it was evening and their plates were cleared and the two men were nailed firmly in place in the grand dining hall by a half-empty bottle of whiskey—again, proclaimed the captain, Prohibition be damned.

As the dinner hour ended, tables were removed from the center of the room to make space for dancing. A jazz band began its preparations on stage. Captain Watson topped off Dooman's glass and filled another for himself. Without money of his own, Dooman was entirely at the mercy of his benefactor. It was, however, an improvement over his state this morning.

"You've certainly had a rough go of it, Gene," Watson empathized.

"It shakes one's faith in one's fellow man. I know I should practice forgiveness, but a civilized society can't function without proper justice."

"Don't you worry about justice. If we find these scoundrels, I'll handle the justice. That's part of the fun of being in command."

"If." That was the operative word. "If." Captain Watson was garrulously drunk and Dooman doubted he would be leaving this chair before sunup. He had seen it before.

Watson raised his glass and encouraged Dooman to raise his own. They drank.

"You shouldn't think they're all like that," the captain continued. "Most on these ships are good boys. Upstanding, God-fearing young men with rare exceptions."

"I don't doubt it, Ed. I'm convinced of it. But that doesn't put me out any less."

Dooman thought of Tokyo and how in the scheme of things his missing wallet was no great tragedy. He had tried contacting the State Department again that afternoon but at this point they preferred he continue his sabbatical rather than return to where he felt most useful.

It wasn't as if he couldn't enjoy himself here. There was lively conversation all around, there was music, there was dance. The people were friendly and full of life. An attractive woman in a red dress caught his eye from across the room and he blushed. Only the unsettled nature of his position held him back from pursuing these opportunities—that, he admitted to himself, along with an innate timidity that seemed to recede with each drink passed to him by the captain, who Dooman now realized was still talking.

"And that's why you should sail with us tomorrow," Watson said, summarizing whatever had come before. This was a surprise. It pulled Dooman from his reverie. "The Navy owes you that much after all you've been through."

"I'm not that drunk yet," Dooman protested, although he wasn't so sure. "I was hoping to keep my feet on dry land for a good while still. And what with the police reports and waiting on a new letter of credit and new identification—I really couldn't."

"You'd be my guest of honor. It's entirely safe, I promise."

"Your kindness is a credit to the United States Navy, Ed, it truly is. You'll make admiral in no time."

Dooman should have declined the offer more forcefully. This was not how he had planned to spend his first days back in America. But Watson was already filling his drink again and Dooman was having trouble thinking that many steps ahead.

"Give it some consideration at least," the captain said, raising his glass and encouraging Dooman to do the same. "We could have your papers forwarded to San Diego. Promise me you'll drink on it."

Dooman took the glass and took a braver swallow than he knew was good for him. His friend was a good man. The alcohol warmed his chest and filled him with a rush of love for all humanity, taking him happily past the point of no return. From across the lobby he spotted a flash of that red dress again and he was sure another smile. Dooman smiled back.

"That's the spirit, Gene," Captain Watson said. "We forget our troubles tonight. Tomorrow we plan the future of the free world."

※※※

They walked together hand in hand. She wore his coat over her shoulders and they leaned together for warmth on this clear, cold autumn night. The lights of countless ships reflected in the still water of the bay.

"I hope you're not terribly disappointed that we didn't get to cheat anyone today," Ruby said.

He squeezed her hand. Nothing could disappoint him tonight. It had all been a ruse anyway, this whole idea of tracking down the man with the wallet. All he had wanted was to spend some time with this girl, to get to know her before his ship sailed. Now that he knew her, that was it for the ship—except for one last thing.

"You're not like the others, are you?" she said. "You're special. I can tell."

"The United States Navy would tell you different."

"They just don't know what to do with someone like you."

"And you do?"

They walked slowly despite the cold. Groups of sailors passed them by, hurrying back to beat the bell. Watching these men, Haines had no second thoughts over his plans. It was not as if there were a war on, and there would be no wars in the future, not for quite some time at least, not after the last one. For Haines the Navy had been just a job, and not a great one. He might as well have been on a factory line or digging coal. He might miss his friends for a while but they would be fine without him. Anything he could do on a ship could be done equally well by other men eager to take his place.

"I have ideas," Ruby said. "Lots of ideas."

He wanted to stop her, to look at her, to kiss her right there, to warm her with an embrace. But he had only a few minutes to spare if he were to accomplish his task before curfew.

"We'll have plenty of time to try them out later," he said.

She told him she had been thinking about getting into the motion picture business. There was a brightness to her, an enthusiasm and light that people would gladly follow. But he knew nothing about movies.

"What's to know?" she said. "Stories are free. You take something from Shakespeare or the Bible. Find a writer to clean it up for you. Hire a cameraman. Actors are cheap. Everybody wants to be an actor. Put a kiss at the end and bang, you're a producer."

Haines was not surprised. This girl was the right girl. "Still, it can't be that easy," he said.

"You didn't learn to palm cards overnight, did you? Any good con takes hard work and planning. You've just got to be smarter than the next guy, and make the next guy think he's smarter than you."

"And that's the movie business?"

"That and knowing who's sleeping with who."

He held her closer as they walked. "I knew you were dangerous," he said.

"A grifter knows a grifter."

"It's like looking in the mirror."

"So what do you say? Partners?"

They stopped at a gate at the foot of a long pier through which only authorized Navy personnel could pass. Several ahead of them strolled for the row of destroyers tied up side by side.

"Just one thing to do first," Emmett said.

"Do you have to?"

He told her there was something he needed from his locker. It had sentimental value, he told her. He told her he would be in and out before she knew it. He kissed her and then headed through the gate, looking back twice to wave.

The planks of the pier rocked beneath his feet with each step, but as at so many moments that day, he felt as if he were walking on air.

The sterns of the great gray warships loomed overhead as he passed one then another and another. He counted them out but he already saw his up ahead, the seventh ship on the right—DD-261, the USS *Delphy*. When he reached it he turned back again. He could see Ruby far behind, too far to make out her expression although he had fixed it in his mind. He waved a third time. He would hurry back.

Haines turned down a side spur of the pier and entered the shadowy space between two destroyers, the *Delphy* and the identical USS *Young*. He climbed the ramp to the deck of his ship and arrived unnoticed, the lax watch probably somewhere on an unauthorized cigarette break.

He entered the aft deckhouse then descended the ladder to the crew quarters, passing a row of bunks and arriving at the lockers. There was plenty of activity in the room with the rest of the evening's late arrivals gearing down, and his presence went unremarked. He had worried about running into Pearson and the others, but they didn't seem to be around. That could be either good news or bad, but he had no time to worry about it.

He opened a locker labeled with his name and pushed aside a bundle of folded clothing. Checking over a shoulder first to make sure he remained unobserved, he pried loose a false flat bottom, revealing stacks of cash—tens and twenties laid out evenly, several thousand dollars worth. He pocketed the money, returned the false bottom, replaced the clothing, and closed the locker's lid.

Haines left the crew quarters without a word to his shipmates and climbed back to the main deck. He made it as far as the ramp when a voice called out behind his back.

"Haines. Where do you think you're going?"

It was Cummings, the ship's chief quartermaster, a solid, competent sailor who had a reputation for being serious but fair. Haines wasn't sure what the man was doing on deck at this hour. Normally the chief would be up front prepping with the navigator, or more likely warm in his bed since tomorrow's run was just a simple trip back home to San Diego. As the chain of command went, though, there were worse he could have run into.

"Liberty's not over yet, is it?"

"You've got ten minutes. What luck do you think you'll have in ten minutes?"

Haines gave the man a sheepish smile. "A whole lot, I hope. I just need to say goodbye to my girl."

"You got a girl, huh?"

"She's the best. She's waiting at the gate."

Cummings softened just enough. "Make it quick," he said. "Not a minute past."

Haines thanked the man and skipped down the ramp, whistling as he went. He was almost to the turn of the pier at the ship's stern when he heard the voices.

"I'm gonna beat his ass. Next time I see him I'll beat his ass."

Haines recognized Pearson and recognized that he was deep into his whiskey. He heard his footsteps stumbling, likely as he lost his balance punching the air.

"You don't quit your team," Grady's voice added. "Whoever you are. You're a sailor for life. It's not right."

And then Forsythe: "There's nothing we can do now. You can't teach him a lesson if you can't find him."

But Haines had no place and no time to hide, so find him they would. Pearson stopped short as he rounded the corner, the two friends now face to face. He held an unopened whiskey bottle in one hand. He had probably swiped it from the bar during an end-of-evening riot.

"Speak of the devil," he said. "Where ya headed, traitor?"

The other two, now that Haines could see their faces, were nearly as drunk as Pearson. They somehow managed to hold one another upright as they stumbled forward.

"When I told you to have fun, Jack, I didn't mean drink the entire bar."

Pearson waved the bottle at him. "I'm not finished yet."

Haines tried to step around his friends but Earl Grady moved to block the way.

"Not so fast, smart guy. Where you going?"

"Come on, Earl. You don't want a fight."

"I'm a sailor in the United States Navy. I live for a fight."

This would not end well. His friends were in the belligerent stage of their intoxication. Haines again tried to step around them but this time Forsythe grabbed his arm.

"Hold up. We just wanna talk. Are you leaving?"

"She's waiting for me."

"Are you leaving?"

It was Pearson this time, in full menace. Haines hesitated but not for long. He could lie to Cummings but he owed his friends the truth.

"Yeah," he said. "I'm leaving."

What happened next seemed to happen in slow motion, although even so Haines was powerless to stop it.

Pearson swung with his free fist, his other still grasping the bottle, and somehow connected with Haines' jaw. Haines stumbled back, knocked free of Forsythe's grip. He shook off the punch and charged Pearson. The others grabbed him from behind, grappling and punching and knocking him over. They began to kick him while he was down.

Traitor. Quitter. Son of a bitch.

Haines lay fetal on the dock, helpless against the barrage. He struggled to rise but every movement made it worse. His mind went to Ruby just out of sight around the corner. She shivered in the cold, waiting, shivering inside his coat. She watched and waited, watched and waited through the night, but the bells have rung, the sailors are gone. Her young man does not return.

SATURDAY

Haines lay battered and bruised in the bed. He was sore all over but warm and content beneath a thick stack of soft blankets. He half-opened one blackened eye.

"Stay with me," Ruby said. "Promise me you'll stay."

"I promise."

She placed her delicate hand on his forehead. She caressed his cheek. He felt the rock of the ship, the rumble of the engines, the shouts of the gunnery crews at their stations running through their drills.

"Load! Commence firing! Silence!"

"Shit," Haines said.

"What's that?" A pharmacist's mate stood just outside the partially screened bunk. "You're awake?"

Haines closed his eyes and looked again inside his head for Ruby. This single wool blanket was anything but soft.

"This feels like a boat," Haines said.

"*Delphy* at your service."

"So I've been shanghaied."

The pharmacists' mate pulled back the screen. "You took a beating," he said. He examined Haines' eyes as he spoke. He prodded his ribs and pulled his limbs. "No lasting damage that I can see. Let me know if any of this hurts."

"How long have I been out, doc?"

"Oh, I'm no doctor. You think the Navy can afford a real doctor? I just read the books and slap the bandages where they tell me."

"It feels like we're at sea. Or maybe that's my concussion."

"We shoved off at 0700. You've been down since your friends brought you in last night."

Haines remembered. "I don't have friends," he said.

The pharmacist's mate checked his paperwork. "Grady, Forsythe, and Pearson, it says. It says here they rescued you from a crowd of drunken civilians. Is that what happened?"

Haines wanted to close his eyes again. He wanted Ruby. "If that's what it says," he replied. "Who can argue with it if the Navy wrote it down?"

⋊⋉⋊⋉

The sun flashed bright on the chop as the flagship *Delphy* led the fourteen ships of Destroyer Squadron 11 in an elegant corpen turn to the south out of San Francisco Bay. In a perfectly executed nautical ballet, DesRon 11 united with the seventeen ships of DesRon 12, already traveling at high speed. The decks of these thirty-one identical Clemson-class destroyers, the pride of the post-war Navy, swarmed with white-uniformed sailors as the two squadrons together performed their battle drills. Gun crews worked fast, hard, and efficiently as they targeted flags on nearby ships. Officers called out commands. "Load! Commence firing! Silence! Carry on! Cease firing! Unload!"

Captain Edward H. Watson beamed with pride as he led his companion, Eugene Dooman, up to the walkway behind the bridge. They paused to survey the activity below and behind on the other ships.

"Heads up, Gene. Isn't that a beautiful sight? These three columns, that's Divisions 31, 32, and 33. DesRon 11. Fourteen ships including the *Delphy,* all under my command."

Dooman looked ill. He was in no condition for conversation but he made the attempt. "It's … quite something, Ed."

They pushed on into the bridge where a huddle of officers was busy at work. The space was unremarkable and spare, highlighted by the panoramic view and the great wheel for steering the ship and the polished brass dial and handle of the Engine Order Telegraph for sending commands to the engine room below. Lt. Cmdr. Donald T. Hunter came forward from the navigation cabin as Chief Quartermaster Cummings scanned the shoreline with binoculars. Lt. Lawrence Blodgett stood by with the young officer of the deck, Ensign Morrow, while a helmsman worked to hold the line as the boat yawed against the northwest winds and the waves pushing the starboard stern.

"Commodore on the bridge," Lieutenant junior grade Lattimore, a radioman, alerted as Watson and Dooman entered the cabin.

"At ease, gentlemen," Watson said. "You're making me proud today. You've all met my old friend, Gene Dooman." Dooman regretted this repeated introduction, regretted this focus on himself. He would have preferred to roll into a ball on the floor of a dark cabin, where he could do solo battle against the state of his gut without these distracting social niceties. Dooman knew he did not belong on the bridge—it had to be a violation of protocol, and he sensed the awkwardness among the junior officers—but Watson had insisted on giving him the full tour. "An unfortunate series of circumstances has landed Gene as our guest for this voyage, so let's show off a little, shall we?"

The men relaxed. Captain Watson was on their side.

"Drills going well, sir?" Hunter asked him.

"Admiral Kittelle won't complain. Conditions are good ahead for our speed run, I take it?"

The forward windows of the bridge offered a bird's eye view of a gunnery crew working a four-inch fifty-caliber Mark 9 gun on the wet deck below, the men seemingly immune to the fast sea spray that threatened to wash them away every time the sharp bow split an overtaken swell. This was a lot to ask of Dooman's stomach so he tried focusing on the wide horizon instead.

"A couple points of concern, sir," replied Blodgett. "There's a steamer run aground off San Miguel Island this morning. The whole channel is socked in with fog."

"Nothing we can't handle," Hunter said.

"And there's been some heavy wave damage in ports to the south. Unusual seas due to all that seismic activity in the western Pacific."

Watson nodded. All routine, all easily managed. "All the better to give our green young men a taste of life at sea," he said.

"Speaking of green, sir—" This was Hunter now, gesturing toward the door at the rear of the bridge as it slammed shut. "It looks like your guest is regretting his choices."

Watson looked back to see Dooman now outside at the walkway, leaning over the railing. The men inside the bridge could just make out the sound as Dooman retched onto the deck below.

"He's a good man," Watson said. "But what good man isn't out of his depth among the ladies of San Francisco?"

Watson's lieutenants, these well traveled veterans of Navy life, fondly recalled their own past encounters, their own painful mornings after.

"He was lucky to make it out alive, Commodore."

XXXXX

Haines tried to stretch out his limbs. They were stiff and they ached but the damage felt superficial. He would be fine.

"I've seen this before," said the pharmacist's mate. "I can't say it's my first time."

"Am I free to go?" Haines was still laid out in the bunk, still under orders not to get up, but he felt restless. There were scores to settle.

"You're free to return to your station if that's what you want. If you still need time to cool down I can recommend KP. Or you can just lie here contemplating the errors of your ways. I guarantee your friends haven't forgotten."

Haines was sure the pharmacist's mate knew more than he let on. "Too late to swim for it, huh?"

"This is the Navy, son. Why swim when there's a perfectly good boat under your feet?"

Haines could think of a few reasons, none of which would be wise to share. He found another when the door to the sick bay opened and the pharmacist's mate snapped to attention as Captain Watson entered. Haines attempted to rise as well but the captain waved them both to relax.

"No need, no need. I hear we've got a battle-hardened hero on the rack." The captain appeared to be in a jovial mood as he stepped forward to take a look at Haines. There was someone else back there as well, someone obscured by the half-drawn curtain. "That's a nice shiner you've got, sailor. I'd hate to see your opponent. A man's got to be a fool to take on the United States Navy."

"I won't argue with that, sir," Haines replied.

The captain turned to the pharmacist's mate. "How are his prospects?"

"I'd say that's mostly up to him, Captain. He seems pretty sharp. He'll be fine as long as he keeps his nose out of trouble from here out."

"I'm sure he will." The captain chuckled as if in on the joke, whatever that joke might be. "Won't you, son?"

"Aye, sir."

"Good to hear. Good to hear." Then the captain turned to the man behind him. "Gene, step inside a bit. For my friend here," he asked the pharmacist's mate, "what would you recommend for a rough morning after?" And then to his friend again: "Or is it a heartache? Which did we decide?"

"Really, Ed, I'm fine. It's just—no offense to the United States Navy—but your *Delphy* rides a little rough."

Watson laughed again. He was in a rare good mood. But Haines reacted instinctively to the sound of a voice he recognized. He rolled to his side to face the bulkhead, careful to do so casually, and feigned continued illness, hoping not to be noticed.

The pharmacist's mate took a bottle from the cupboard and shook out a couple of tablets. "If it's liquor or a woman," he said, "the best advice I can give is another shot of what ails you. Short of that, aspirin is on the menu."

Dooman accepted the pills gratefully, glancing as he did so at the patient on the bunk but seeing only the bandaged back of the man's head. "You're very kind," he said.

Haines could almost feel the breath of the new men pushed into this cramped cabin, invading his safe space. He was unsure whether he needed to hide. His misconduct had been minor, only borderline illegal, and he had been out of uniform. The man would probably not recognize him, but that was no reason to avoid caution.

"Mr. Dooman here had a run-in with some rather unsavory young sailors who stole his wallet," the captain explained. "We're doing all we can to make it up to him today."

Now this was news. Haines sank himself further into the bed, willing himself to invisibility if only it were possible. Of all the unsavory young sailors he knew, and he knew a few, he narrowed the pool of suspects with the opportunity and the inclination to three, and to one in particular—one reckless, drunken lout whose selfish greed now seemed to have put them all in danger.

"That's a shame, Captain," the pharmacist's mate said. "Did you catch the men?"

"As of yet, no. But if you hear anything, you'll be sure to report it?"

"Aye, sir."

"Well that's that, then. Carry on, gentlemen, and keep up the good work."

Watson led Dooman out of the sick bay but Haines could still hear them as they departed the corridor.

"A good captain always knows what's happening on board his ship, Gene. He inspires his men, and yet he doesn't get in the way of them doing their jobs. That's my philosophy."

"And a good one at that, Ed. It's no wonder they love you so."

When they were clear Haines turned away from the bulkhead again. If there had been any doubts about how he would respond to the events of the previous evening, he pushed them aside. Caution had served him well, and he would continue to be cautious for the rest of the voyage. But now there was something he needed to do.

"Friends of yours?" the pharmacist's mate asked, nodding toward their departed captain and Dooman. He watched Haines with a curious expression.

"I don't have friends," Haines said.

XOXOX

Haines checked himself out of sick bay in time to join his next scheduled shift. The battle drills had ended and a calm had returned to the ship. Off to starboard and a bit to stern he could see on the horizon the silhouettes of the seventeen ships of DesRon 12 falling behind as they veered toward deeper water. The *Delphy*, meanwhile, led its own squadron in a straight column headed south along the coast. They sailed in full sun but a bank of fog had already begun to obscure the shore to port. All that was none of Haines' business, though, as he took one last breath of fresh salt air and headed below.

In the crew quarters he opened his locker. Sitting on top of his folded uniform he found Pearson's unopened bottle of whiskey. Was this a peace offering or a setup? Whatever it was, it compounded the risk. Whatever it was, Haines wasn't having it.

"Jack, you idiot."

He looked around the quarters to verify that no one was paying attention, then he pulled the cash from his pockets and slipped it beneath the locker's false bottom. He buried the whiskey, which would not fit with the money, under his spare clothes. It would have to do for now until he could find a better hiding place or better yet smuggle it topside and lose it over a rail.

Changing into his work blues was a somewhat futile gesture—not because of the stiffness of his aching limbs, although that made things difficult, but because as soon as he entered the engine room he was ready to take them off again. It was a world of hot pipes, valves, gauges, and polished brass, all spotless despite the shimmering black oil in the giant pistons. The room was two levels high, with the upper level being a walkway that circumnavigated the space, its floor nothing but a metal grating so that the top was visible from the bottom, and vice versa.

Haines descended a ladder to the lower level, where he removed his blue shirt, stripping down to a white undershirt like the rest of the men working below. The heat in the place was oppressive. The room was also loud with the rhythmic drone of the engines. The men had to raise their voices to be heard and remind themselves not to take offense at being yelled at.

"Look who decided to join us from his vacation," shouted Lieutenant Cruzen, the lead engineer.

"Sick bay was a suitable punishment for my sins, sir," Haines replied.

"I'm sure they're weighing heavy on your soul. Ready to get back to work?"

"I'm a changed man, sir."

The lieutenant was skeptical of that. "Give it a rest, Haines. Your band of monkeys is in the fire room."

"Jack's in there?"

"Started him in the bilge today. He's a changed man, too."

Haines started forward down a passageway toward the boilers.

"Haines," the lieutenant called out with one last bit of advice. "Whatever's going on, it's best it doesn't go any further."

Was it that obvious? Haines prided himself on his straight poker face, although that face today hinted his secrets in unmistakable black and blue. "Not a problem, sir," he said. "I learned my lesson."

He passed the entrance to the first boiler room then stopped beside the second. The access light told him it was clear to enter the airlock, and so he did. He shut the first hatch behind himself and stood there in that tight space for a few deep breaths. Then he opened a second hatch and entered the pressurized boiler room.

If the engine room was the heart of the ship, this place was its fiery soul. The massive boiler seemed to breathe a sigh of welcome as Haines arrived—hello to an old friend—as it went about its business of converting water to steam, the life force flowing through a complicated series of pipes and valves that kept the boat alive. Working here was like working in an oven, a critical job entrusted to four men: Grady, Forsythe, Pearson, and Haines. There were three other boiler rooms on board, although under normal conditions no more than two operated at a time, with several shifts rotating through the day.

Sweating profusely as soon as he entered the space, Haines peeled off his undershirt. His body was bruised from the night before but he wore the purple as a badge of honor. The other men were already stripped to their waists. Grady controlled the air supply as Forsythe fed fuel to the burner and Pearson logged notes. They stopped what they were doing as Haines shut and latched the hatch and stepped up to Pearson.

"Take them off," Haines said.

It could have been the heat, the hangover, or his time in the bilge, but whatever the reason, even knowing what was coming, Pearson removed his eyeglasses and stood without objection, without even a defensive stance. Whatever the reason, Pearson stood and took it as Haines sent a right cross hard to his jaw, knocking him to the floor.

"I owed you that," Haines said.

Pearson rubbed his face. He sat up, stood, and put his glasses back on.

"It wasn't personal, Em."

"Go to hell."

Haines had been ready for a fight, had been ready to work this out as gentlemen do. But Pearson seemed subdued. Maybe that bottle of whiskey had been an apology after all. Maybe he felt guilty over what he had done. Or maybe he was just too hung over to care.

"You're on the water gauge," Pearson said, turning his attention to the logbook.

Haines went to the gauge. It was the most boring job in the world—just stare at the water level and turn a valve if it got too high or too low. But the atmosphere remained tense. He noticed the ache from the punch spreading through his knuckles.

"It was for your own good, Emmett," Henry Forsythe said at last. "You're a United States Navy sailor and a Navy sailor never jumps his post. He never abandons his crew."

"Some day you'll understand," Grady added. "Some day you'll thank us for this."

"Are you really that stupid, Earl?"

"Be grateful we got to you first. You want five years for desertion? We couldn't let you do that to yourself."

"What I do's got nothing to do with you."

"We're a team, Em," Forsythe said. "We need to be able to trust each other. That's how we stay alive."

Haines knew a con when he heard one, even when it came straight from a Navy training manual. "Trust is for people who haven't had their ribs kicked in," he said. "And what about you, Jack? Are you someone these fellas can trust?"

Pearson said nothing. Either he didn't want to talk to Haines or he didn't want to answer the question.

)()()(

All things considered, Eugene Dooman wished he were dead. His head throbbed as every beat of his heart tried to push his brain out of his skull. His stomach rose and fell, not at all in time with the ship, as whatever was left inside him sloshed around searching for a way out. He wished he had never gotten on board. He wished he had not agreed to those last few drinks.

He sat in the chair at the captain's desk, alone in his friend's quarters. He was grateful that the room had a separate toilet. He counted the number of movements it would take to reach it, rehearsing every footstep in his mind. He imagined himself as one of those samurai he had read about, running through death to strike his final blows with the momentum of will. He laid his head on the desk, rolled it onto his left temple, and wished again for sweet release.

On the bulkhead facing him he saw a telephone for onboard communication, backed up by an array of speaking tubes. He heard muffled voices through the bulkheads.

"I wasn't there, but I heard it from my friend Davey Thompson, who was."

"Commodore really tore into Captain Roper. No readings, he said. No soundings."

"He's wanting to set some speed records today. We're practicing engines, he says, not navigation."

"They do things by the book on the *Kennedy*. Pity for them."

Dooman heard the click of the latch and saw the turn of the handle as the cabin door swung in and open. He raised himself to another shot of sharp, lingering pain and nausea. Captain Watson stepped inside, followed by an older Filipino man in the uniform of a cabin cook.

"Here he is, Sofronio," the captain said. "Still suffering the aftereffects of last night."

The cook, Sofronio Dalida, carried a tray of scalloped potatoes, fried eggs, and sausage. He placed it on the desk before Dooman, who tried not to make a face at the food. It was both the only thing and the last thing he wanted.

"Do yourself a favor, Eugene, put this down. It's an old sailor's remedy."

"Listen to your captain," added Dalida. "He's a good man. He's a smart man."

Watson patted the cook on the back and sent him on his way.

"I know it doesn't feel like it," Captain Watson continued to Dooman, "but you're lucky to be on board today. This is an historic occasion for the squadron."

Dooman stared at the food without touching it. He feared the consequences. "So I've heard," he said.

This confused the captain at first, but then the distant voices cut through the silence again: "Still, you should have seen Roper. Beet red, and it looked like the commodore was about to eat his face off. They got into it."

Watson laughed at that. "So you've discovered the acoustic advantage of my cabin. I always know what my men are up to."

Dooman in his illness was confused by the captain's good mood. "Are you not concerned to hear them talk about you like that?" he asked.

"I'd rather hear them than not. My crew loves me and they fear me. It's the best of both worlds."

Dooman could not help but admire his old friend. "You'll be an admiral in no time," he said.

"After we finish today's run, I don't see how anyone could object."

)O(O(

The day wore on uneventfully as days at sea often do. The ships of DesRon 11 streamed at twenty knots through worsening seas. They raced in single column formation according to longstanding Navy tradition, the flagship *Delphy* leading the *SP Lee*, the *Young*, the *Woodbury*, the *Nicholas*, the *Farragut*, the *Fuller*, the *Percival*, the *Somers*, the *Chauncey*, the *Kennedy*, the *Paul Hamilton*, the *Stoddert*, and the *Thompson*, worthy ships all with worthy crew and command. This was a routine run but there was nothing these sleek greyhounds of the sea could not handle. They knifed through the swells, pitching and rolling and yawing as waves crashed over bows and sterns rose to lift surging propellers clear of the water.

Down in the combined crew quarters and mess of the *Delphy*, Haines, Grady, Forsythe, and Pearson ate with other sailors at the end of their shift, all of them tilting in unison with the motion of their enclosed world. The meal consisted mostly of glop ladled onto a plate, which the hungry men enjoyed more than they cared to admit.

Our four, though, ate in a silence that was equal parts awkward and aggressive, their shipmates leaving them to it. Pearson sulked. Grady tried to broker a peace by suggesting a card trick. Haines told him where he could put the deck. Forsythe mused that temperatures were cooler in the boiler room.

They could not have known what was coming. They could not have known their small part in it or how they might have changed things. They saw only their own place in this play, only the space contained within their own four walls, their own minutes and hours. Events on the bridge and in their captain's quarters went unregarded, irrelevant to the conflict at hand. Haines held close the news of the hunt for the stolen wallet, unsure whether any advantage gained by sharing the information outweighed the escalation sure to come if he were to accuse Pearson of the crime.

Things could have ended differently. They could have worked together to get rid of the evidence. They could have tossed the wallet and moved the money. The whiskey and the cards could have found their way into the ocean. But at this point the cogs had come off the machine and the machine lurched unchecked, uncontrolled, full speed toward its fate.

Haines thought of Ruby shivering in his jacket at the foot of the pier. She could not have known why he left her there. She could not have known where he was headed now. She could not have known that he would never arrive.

1600 HOURS

On the bridge of the *Delphy*, Lieutenant Commander Hunter felt the yaw of the ship and warned the helmsman to mind his rudder. Lieutenant Blodgett scanned shoreward with binoculars. The sky was mostly clear above with clouds ahead, and the bank of fog to port showed no signs of thinning. It had been with them all day, causing them to miss every navigational landmark from Point Año Nuevo on down.

Lattimore brought news from the radio room: "We've got more on that civilian wreck off San Miguel Island. When they struck the reef this morning they'd been in heavy fog for three days."

"We're in for it all the way, then," Hunter replied. "At twenty knots it'll be a good time."

"Should we update the commodore?" Blodgett framed the suggestion as a question, but Hunter brushed it off.

"He'll pop in when he wants to know more."

"He sure is in a good mood today," Lattimore said.

"He's got politicians to show off to."

This terrified the junior radioman. "How can you talk about him behind his back like that? He hears everything."

Despite his growing apprehension over the ship's course, Blodgett joined Hunter for a laugh at Lattimore's expense just as Watson and his friend Dooman arrived on the bridge.

"Don't say anything you'll regret and you'll be fine," Hunter advised the radioman. "Make sure you mention his fine taste in women and whiskey every once in a while."

"And also," added Captain Watson, "my love of literature and my peculiar fascination with the rise and fall of ancient Mesopotamian civilizations."

"How could we forget?"

Watson loved the warm welcome. He relaxed in the admiration of his men. Even Dooman managed a smile, the passage of time having somewhat eased the symptoms of his overindulgence.

"You should know, sir," Hunter continued, more seriously now, "we're hearing a lot of chatter from the other ships."

"Roper still?"

"He'd like to break off Division 32 to join the search for survivors of that wrecked steamer."

"He still wants to slow for soundings, doesn't he? It's not about the search. He's afraid of navigating the channel."

Blodgett took this as his opening. "We do have several discrepancies, sir." He directed Watson's attention to a nautical chart and pointed out locations as he spoke. "Because of the fog we haven't been able to take a shore sighting since Pigeon Point at 1130 hours. But RDF bearings put us here."

Hunter scoffed. As a navigator with wartime experience and even time as an instructor at Annapolis, he had little faith in shore-based Radio Direction Findings, especially when compared with tried and true methods that sailors had relied on for centuries. "There's not a chance we're that far north," he said. "Not at the speeds we've been running."

The captain winked at his friend—this is how it's done, Eugene, he seemed to say—as he stepped into the role of thoughtful decision maker: "So what's your take, Don?"

Hunter fingered the chart well south of Blodgett's estimate. "Dead reckoning calculations based on bearing and speed over the last five hours have us well past Piedras Blancas already. We're making great time. But if we pay attention to that damned RDF station, they'll run us hard into San Miguel Island—just like that steamer."

Assured by the easy solution and the confidence of his man, Watson turned to Dooman. "What did I tell you, Gene? When you let officers this talented do what they're trained to do, they barely need my help."

Hunter stood tall, pleased with his victory.

Blodgett, however, remained unconvinced. "Helmsman," he cautioned, "mind your rudder."

XOXOX

Haines leaned against the port rail, back to the wind, protecting a lit cigarette. He had come up from the aft crew quarters, through the aft deckhouse, and strolled forward past two sets of torpedo tubes to the shadow of the rearmost of the four stacks. He stood there at the rail, only partly protected from the wind by the midship deckhouse ahead. The pharmacist's mate came up from below and joined him.

"I'd have thought you'd be in hiding."

"I thought I was. Who'd be fool enough to ride this rail otherwise?"

Haines cupped and lit a second cigarette and gave it to the pharmacist's mate. They looked together toward the wall of gray shrouding the coast.

"Still thinking of that swim?"

Haines studied the cold, sharp waves. Distances at sea could be deceptive but even if he could manage it under warmer, calmer conditions, the hypothermia would surely do him in today. There were easier ways to leave a boat.

"I don't know how you guys do it down there," the pharmacist's mate tried again. "I'd melt."

"The heat's the least of it. It's the company that gets you in the end."

"Those bruises will heal sooner than your pride, I think."

"They left me my hands." Haines studied them front and back, cigarette between thumb and forefinger. He could do a lot with these hands. He had trained them for years in the art of quick, subtle manipulation of the cards. He knew everything they could do and everything they could not. He felt the cold wind against them, felt the slight numbness creeping in, and knew exactly how much it would affect his performance, exactly how he would need to compromise his act. "They do seem to value my hands," he said. "But as long as they're mine, I'm in control."

The pharmacist's mate was not so sure about that.

"Do you really think any of us are in control?"

"I only know about me. And them. And how that's going to end."

They stared together into the ocean and fog. They were alone on deck with nothing to keep them company but the wind whistling the guy-lines. Even those seabirds that never came to land but sometimes followed the ships had given up the chase and peeled away, finding nothing of use in this chain of rigid steel leviathans so intent on splitting the waters and leaving only the churn behind.

At last the pharmacist's mate spoke as much to himself as to Haines. "I was in the war," the man said. "Not the Navy, not a soldier. I drove an ambulance."

The words came softly as if it didn't matter whether they were heard or not. Haines had known other veterans of the ground war in Europe and they weren't generally the type to tell tales—at least not the men who had tales worth telling. Haines had learned to let them talk in their own time, to listen and to learn, to take these rare confessions as gifts. Sometimes the stories were useful. What had Ruby said about stories? Maybe there would be a movie in it. He watched an unmoored patch of kelp slip past the ship and grew conscious of the wind burn on his right cheek.

"It was worse than this, this gray," the pharmacist's mate continued. "Sometimes fog, sometimes smoke and fumes. You couldn't see your hand in front of your face. And then it would clear and there were people on their knees trying to separate the parts of men from the parts of horses. Trying to find anything still alive in that mud. It didn't matter what anybody did, how they tried to fight it. Whether they did it alone or together. Nothing lived through that."

He threw his half-finished cigarette over the rail, the orange tip dying in its arc before it reached the water.

"Nobody lived through that," he said. "Not even me. And yet here I am. Talking to you. Trying to figure out if you're worth saving."

⬦⬦⬦

Blodgett again pressed his point to Captain Watson on the bridge. "Captain, it wouldn't be difficult to let the trailing ship from Division 32 slow for soundings. They could report back and rejoin us without slowing the squadron."

For the first time Watson flashed a bit of frustration.

"Are you the navigator on this ship, Lieutenant?"

"I was, sir, until yesterday."

"But you've stepped aside to let the more experienced officer handle those duties."

"With respect, sir—"

Watson cut him off. "Enough, Lieutenant."

Dooman shifted uncomfortably, a reluctant witness to this dressing down. "I'll step outside, Ed," he offered. He left the bridge and descended to the deck below and passed out of the cold into the midship deckhouse.

⬦⬦⬦

"I liked the Navy," Haines told the pharmacist's mate. "I did. I joined because I wanted to be a sailor. I wanted to see the world."

"That's the life."

The sun still shone above somewhere, although it had become hard to spot through the thickening haze that moistened their hands and cheeks at twenty knots. Haines could have gone below. It was past time for any man who valued his comfort. But below were his friends—rather his enemies—and the surging deck and sea spray seemed preferable to that. Also now, he felt a need to justify himself to this pharmacist's mate, this fortuitous confessor, and this came harder than expected.

"We moved around a lot when I was a kid," Haines continued, "if you consider up and down the Mississippi a lot. I learned cards from my father and my uncle. But now I've seen Alaska. I've seen Panama. I've seen Hawaii. And that's all great."

"But?"

"But everywhere I go it's the same people. It never changes, no matter the port. It's always the same dumb sailors with the same dumb ideas."

"That's the life."

They stared down into the water. It was nothing they hadn't seen before, which helped explain why they stood alone. No other sailors loitered on deck. Those few passing by on their duties felt no need to linger.

"It's not even that I dislike them," Haines said. "I don't. I didn't. They were my friends, love 'em or hate 'em. But

I started thinking a while back. I started thinking there had to be something better."

"Better friends?"

"A better me."

"There's the rub."

"I'm good at what I do. I'm good at separating a man from his money, at least in small amounts. But I get the feeling I could be good at something bigger. Something more important."

"And heating a warship isn't it?"

Haines rested within his memories of the past twenty-four hours. He thought of Ruby and the thought calmed him, even while admitting that he barely knew her. He wondered how long he could keep her in his mind's eye, this woman he had left behind.

"I met this girl. I don't know, maybe it wasn't about the girl, even. It could have been anybody. I've still got two years on my commitment and I don't mind waiting it out. But these friends of mine—my friends, they think they were trying to help."

Before Haines could get to the heart of the matter, though, before he could work through all his conflicting thoughts, everything changed. All his worry became ir-relevant in an instant as Eugene Dooman stepped from the deckhouse and in a shock of recognition knew he had found his man.

"You," Dooman said.

Haines tried to hide his surprise. He reverted to his personable, showy routine, working the audience. "Now here's a trick," he said. "A civilian on a Navy ship."

"You thought you'd escaped me."

"I never expected you to track me down at sea," Haines replied, "But a magician still can't reveal his secrets."

He tried to read the man. Clearly he had misjudged him already, never having expected to find him strolling the exposed deck under these conditions. Could Haines talk his way through this, whatever this was? What did this Dooman know, or even worse what did he think he knew?

Dooman, though, was in no mood for games. "You'll reveal a lot more than that before this trip is over."

"I hope you don't expect me to pull a rabbit out of my cap. That would be against regulations."

The door to the deckhouse opened again and from the corner of his eye Haines glimpsed an officer's uniform. It was Cummings, the quartermaster, who had been charitable to him only last night but from whom he expected no mercy now. With more time Haines might have been able to make a case for himself. But there would be no more time.

Dooman smiled the smile of a man with right on his side and the might of the entire United States Navy backing him up. "I'm sure regulations mean little to such a lawless ruffian as yourself," he said. Then he waved the officer over to their little group. "Sir, I demand you arrest this man immediately."

And so it was done.

1700 HOURS

It took a while to sort out the charges and collect the evidence but it wasn't long before Haines found himself escorted to the captain's cabin. He stood at attention as Watson paced the small room, Dooman with his back to the door, a satisfied witness to both the crime and the interrogation.

"This is an outrage. This insult will not stand."

Haines knew not to speak unless asked to do so. He could see laid out on the captain's desk a dozen decks of playing cards, a large stack of cash, and a bottle of whiskey.

"I run a tight ship," exclaimed Captain Watson. "I'm harsh but fair. In this case, I expect I'll be quite harsh. Do you care to explain this? From a false bottom in your locker, no less."

But before Haines could reply, Dooman had his own say. "That's more money than I lost, Ed. Perhaps he had multiple victims."

"Sailor?"

"I'd tell you I'm an honest man, Captain, but what honest man needs to say it? The only thing I took from Mr. Dooman was thirty dollars, which he offered up willingly."

The captain wasn't having it. "What's all this, then?"

"Props for my personal life, sir?"

Haines knew the moment he said it that he had gone too far. Watson slammed his fist to the table.

"You have no personal life. You are a sailor in the United States Navy. You serve your country. You follow orders. You respect the uniform. You live by the grace of your commanding officer. And right now I'm feeling less than graceful."

"Sir. I can explain the cards." Haines scrambled for the right words, but he wasn't sure any right words existed to clear this situation. "I can explain the money. I can't explain the bottle." No matter how he felt about his friends, no matter how they had let him down, there was still a code. He wouldn't turn on them to the brass.

"So it's another one of your magic tricks, then? I've heard about those."

"I'd be more than happy to make it disappear, Captain, if you'd like."

Watson could not hide his disappointment. "Don't you worry about that. You won't be seeing it again. What I'm more concerned with is how a low-ranking enlisted sailor comes by a stack of money bigger than his yearly salary."

"It's my savings, sir."

"You don't earn enough to have a savings."

"I'm industrious, sir."

"Too good for the Navy, are you?"

Haines held his words close. They had been no help so far. They only seemed to make things worse.

"You're a thief and you've stolen from the wrong man," the captain said. "You've stolen from a dear friend of your own captain. Twenty years ago I could have had you keel hauled for less. I still might." He turned and shouted at the cabin door—"Chief Cummings!"— causing Dooman to instinctively step to one side.

The door opened and Haines' arresting officer entered the cabin.

"Get him out of my sight," Watson commanded. "Put him in the brig. And bring me Dalida."

Dalida, already waiting on the captain's command, stepped inside as Cummings escorted Haines from the cabin.

"Two glasses, Sofronio. And ice." The captain looked to his friend Dooman with grim satisfaction. "A bit late for your hair of the dog, but I could use a swig of distraction. I hope you don't mind."

XOXOX

The fast-blown fog had swallowed the sky by the time Cummings escorted Haines aft along the deck. Waves slammed the hull below.

"It's getting rough out there," Haines said.

"It's about to get a lot rougher for you, sorry to say."

They entered the midship deckhouse and climbed below, walking down a passage to a small containment cell. Haines stepped inside as Cummings shut the barred door.

"Do me a favor, Haines. Don't make me look bad."

Cummings turned the lock and left Haines to sit listening to the drone of the engines and the muffled voices of men just out of sight. Haines took a seat on a narrow bunk, reached into a hidden pocket of his uniform, and pulled out a fresh deck of playing cards. He began to shuffle, practicing his usual flourishes: springs and waterfalls and charlier cuts.

He split his attention between the feel of the cards in his fingertips and the vibration of the ship against his back as it powered through the sea at twenty knots. He imagined the touch of the entire world transmitted through steel and ocean. He felt the sand and volcanic rock that cupped the water below reaching out to become high dry land, kelp and grass rooted to hold it together, footsteps upon it breaking pods and stalks, flowers and seeds set free in the wind. He closed his eyes and could see an outcrop of reef rising above the surface, passing the ship at only one hundred yards distance—close, perhaps too close at this speed. He should warn someone. Who could he warn? Who would listen?

Twenty knots. They would be in San Diego by morning. He would be transferred to a holding cell at the shipyard. He would be given a cursory trial. The evidence was overwhelming. It was his word against a gentleman's. He would have an appointed defender, but that was a formality. How long would the sentence be? They might let him send letters, but where would he send them? He had never asked for her address. By the time he saw daylight again she would be gone into a life without him, his own small presence a forgotten footnote.

1815 HOURS

The sun dropped below the horizon without fanfare, without witness, a last missed chance for those below deck who could not be bothered to dress against the cold, to climb the ladders, to brave the miserable spray for a sight they had seen many times before and had every reason to believe they would see many times again. Even for those on the bridge the end of the day arrived almost unnoticed, unremarkable, just a slow dimming of distant light unsourced by diffuse sea smoke. Lieutenant Blodgett peered into the gloom outside, seeing little through glass dense with condensation.

"Relax, Larry," Hunter said, calm in the authority of command. "We'll make the channel soon enough."

"Not if we hit something first."

"Would you be happier with the commodore on the bridge?"

Blodgett knew he wouldn't. "His good mood is gone."

"What did Haines do, anyway?" Hunter asked.

"Who knows? It's Haines. He probably made an elephant disappear. I'm not sure it was a good idea to bring this Dooman on board."

"No second guessing your superiors, Lieutenant. That's not your job."

Blodgett bit his tongue on that one—somebody needed to do some second guessing around here. He was saved from an unfortunate reply when Lattimore arrived with an update.

"More crosstalk from Division 32," he said. "They've called for RDF bearings again."

Blodgett moved to the chart, eager for the results. "What did they get?"

"Who cares what they got?" Hunter interrupted. "We've had faulty RDF results all day long. Division 32 knows they've got one simple job, and that's to follow our lead and match our speed."

2024 HOURS

"How does it come to this, Gene? how does a good man take such a wrong turn?" Watson stared morosely at the melting ice in his glass. The bottle of liquor confiscated from Haines sat half empty nearby.

"Temptation is always with us, Ed." Dooman stared at his empty glass. He knew temptation all too well—his stomach had only just recovered from the previous night. This latest glass seemed to have helped but he declined his friend's offer of a refill as Captain Watson helped himself to another. Dooman had lost track of how many that made for the captain.

"We try to do right by these boys. We know they don't often come from the best of circumstances. But we give them a new family. An upright family with honest rules and values. We feed them, we clothe them, we teach them. We offer them a way. And even then sometimes it just doesn't work out."

"You can't take it personally, Ed," Dooman advised.

"How can I not? I dedicate my life to my crew. Betrayal hurts." He shook his head, shot down his drink, and poured another. He sat quietly, letting the alcohol do its best. And then: "John Donne," he said.

"What?"

"No man is an island. You know it. John goddamn Donne."

It was clear to Dooman that his friend was drunk now and starting to ramble.

"No man is an island, entire of itself," Watson recited from memory. "Every man is a piece of the continent, a part of the main." He took a deep breath and enunciated the words as if he were on stage, growing louder and brasher with each line. "If a clod be washed away by the sea, Europe is the less, as well as if a promontory were, as well as if a manor of thy friend's, or of thine own were. Any man's … any man's …"

He had begun to lose the thread and was therefore grateful when a bell rang summoning him to the bridge.

"Fuck it," he said. "That bell's for me."

Captain Watson rose unsteadily, leaving Dooman alone in the cabin. He climbed to the bridge hand over hand on the rail to steady himself against the rolling of the ship or maybe the rolling in his brain, only to find himself back in the storm of discord among his lieutenants.

"Sir, we really need to take a closer look at these latest Radio Direction Findings." It was Blodgett again, back on that beaten horse. "If they're correct and we rely on our dead reckoning estimates instead, it puts the entire squadron in jeopardy."

"RDF again? Who authorized more RDF?"

"Captain Roper took it upon himself, sir."

"Roper's been a thorn in my ass all day."

"I'm sorry about that, sir, but look at the chart. If the RDF is correct, we're still well north of Point Arguello. We'll hit the coast if we turn too soon."

Hunter, again, had heard enough. "The RDF is not correct. My calculations put us thirty minutes from the channel. If we keep this bearing as Lieutenant Blodgett suggests, we'll smash into San Miguel Island."

"I'm not saying your math is wrong," Blodgett replied, tamping down his frustration. "But it's been nine hours since our last fixed position. Relying on propeller speed for calculations in these wind and current conditions, that's a lot of unknown variables to throw us off. And when we've got these RDF numbers—"

"Dammit, Lieutenant, I've been doing this for twenty years. Your damned radio is no match for a real navigator with a sextant. I know how to do my job."

All this bickering was a blur to Captain Watson, just petty arguments and grudges that had nothing to do with him. "Enough," he said. "I've had enough discord within the ranks for one day." He addressed Hunter directly. "Commander, the ship is yours. I trust your judgment and experience. If you say we should make the turn at 2100 hours, then at 2100 hours we make the turn."

"Thank you, Commodore," Hunter replied. Then he gave the order to Lattimore to notify the other ships. "Follow our lead and we'll shoot straight into the channel."

2055–2109 HOURS

Ruby came to Haines in the darkness of his cell.

"This is a fine mess," she said.

"We play the hand we're dealt," he replied aloud to the silence. He shuffled the cards and dealt a hand to himself, eyes closed, doing it all by feel as he let his imagination take him away. They sat on the bed in her apartment, a mess of cards between them, picking them up together one at a time and returning them to an ordered pile.

"That doesn't sound like the best way to win a game. Shouldn't you just deal yourself a winning hand?"

"Sometimes you have to lose to win," he said. "That's the setup. You know how it works."

He pictured Jack Pearson restless in his bunk just a few spaces away.

"A girl's gotta do what a girl's gotta do," she had told him. "A grifter knows a grifter."

Pearson took a wallet from his pocket and opened it to stare at a large stack of bills inside.

"You hold back," Haines said. "You let them think they've got the upper hand. You let them think they're conning you."

※※

In the captain's cabin, Dooman took his glass and the captain's to the sink and emptied them both. He picked up the half-empty bottle and then, hesitating only a moment, poured that liquor down the drain as well.

※※

"But it doesn't always work, does it?" Ruby asked. "What do you do then? When you're outplayed or caught or outgunned or your luck just plain turns bad?"

※※

In the engine room the machinists made their rounds. There wasn't a lot to do after a dozen hours at a steady speed, just monitor the fluid levels and watch for warning signs and write notes in the logs.

※※

"Do you always have a backup plan? Do you always know the quickest way out of any room?"

※※

Blodgett stared nervously into the dark ahead as Hunter gave the order and the helmsman turned the wheel.

※※

"Do you get tired of living three steps ahead of everyone else? Is that how it's always going to be?"

※※

The *Delphy* turned eastward. One by one the ships in a line behind it turned as well, any drift from falling out of formation entirely unnoticed in the thickening fog.

※※

"Yes," said Haines.
"No," said Haines.
"Maybe," said Haines.
And Ruby: "Come back to me, Emmett."
"I will."

※※

The USS *Young*, third in line behind the flagship USS *Delphy* but steering a parallel course offset some twenty yards to starboard, was the first to strike ground, its hull scraping alongside a reef, a gash ripping open at the waterline. With the ship traveling at twenty knots the rocks acted as a ramp, launching the entire destroyer into the air, fuel oil gushing from its side as it slammed back down. The officers on the bridge of the *Young*, Captain Calhoun among them, were thrown from their feet. They struggled to stand as the ship continued ahead, momentum and engines versus solid ground. The shriek of tearing metal reverberated through the bulkheads.

"Lieutenant, report," the captain said. But before anyone could reply, the ship began to list rapidly to starboard.

"All hands on deck! Sound the alarm!"

The *Young's* sirens blared. Captain Calhoun moved the Engine Order Telegraph from FULL AHEAD to STOP.

XXX

In a span of only seconds from the *Young's* impact, the *Delphy* found its own reef just short of a looming cliff. The collision threw Lieutenant Blodgett forward into the bridge window. Hunter slammed hard into the helm but kept his footing. Captain Watson rolled across the floor in a graceless, tumbling, drunken heap.

Lattimore was the first to speak, responding to stunned silence. "Captain? Lieutenant?" But no reply came. Blodgett held a hand to his forehead, pressing to stem the flow of blood into his eyes. Hunter stood in shock as the magnitude of his mistake sank in. Watson just lay there confused, wondering when he had fallen from bed.

Then they heard an immense, twisting, scraping noise as the USS *SP Lee* hit ground off their port.

※※※

In the engine room of the *Delphy* the men picked themselves up from the floor, muttering confusion.

"Silence," commanded Lieutenant Cruzen, the lead engineer.

The crew ceased their talking as they stood, alert and fearful, listening to the roar of the engines and feeling the unusual shaking of the deck beneath their feet. The officer put his hand to the throttle and looked ahead to the Engine Order Telegraph, where the command continued to read FULL AHEAD.

※※※

The scene was much different in the identical engine room of the nearby listing USS *Young*. Alarm bells sounded throughout the ship as the room slowly tilted to starboard, the crew scrambling to stay standing on the shifting floor as water rushed in forcefully from the starboard passage.

"Fuel tanks are ruptured," shouted the lead engineer on duty. "Shut down those boilers now or this whole ship burns."

〉〈〉〈〉〈

One hundred yards west of the sinking *Young*, the destroyer *Woodbury* continued unaware through the fog until it slammed into a small island of rocks jutting up from the sea. On the landward side, a bit behind the grounded *Lee*, the USS *Nicholas* beached full speed onto the rocky shore.

〉〈〉〈〉〈

Blodgett stood, wiped his forehead with his hand, and looked at the smear of blood.

"Alert the trailing ships," he told radio operator Lattimore. "Slow and veer west, everybody."

"Radio's out, Lieutenant. I think we've lost the tower."

"Well get it up," Blodgett commanded, filling the void left by his superior officers. "And sound the sirens to warn them off."

Lattimore and fellow radioman Lieutenant Tipsword left the bridge on the double as Captain Watson rose at last and made his way to the Engine Order Telegraph. He took hold of the lever and pulled the indicator from FULL AHEAD to FULL STERN.

"Sir?" Blodgett inquired.

)O(O(

The EOT alarm sounded in the *Delphy's* engine room as the indicator switched to FULL STERN.

"Full stern," bellowed Lieutenant Cruzen, and the crew sprang into action. But with the change in the engines came an ominous creaking from the hull. The officer tried the ship's intercom. "Bridge, this is the engine." There came no reply as the ship's power flickered off and then back on. He tried the speaking tubes, getting only silence in return. "Bridge, are you hearing me?"

)O(O(

"Sir?" Blodgett repeated. Captain Watson stood in a daze, his hand still on the EOT. So Blodgett turned to Hunter. "Don, we don't know the hull's integrity."

This shook the lieutenant commander from his stupor. Hunter gently pried Captain Watson's hand from the EOT.

"There's still time," Watson said. "We can still get her off this reef."

But Hunter shook his head. No, we can't.

Watson did not object as Hunter moved the indicator to STOP.

)O(O(

The engine room greeted this next change in the EOT with relief.

"Shut her down," Cruzen ordered.

Again the men sprang into action. The officer moved the EOT response dial to STOP, acknowledging compliance. The engine fell silent and the shaking ceased, but the ominous moaning and creaking of the hull continued. The men held their positions, as if afraid the slightest movement might cause the ship to break apart.

"I'm not liking this, Lieutenant," one man noted.

"Neither am I, sailor. Neither am I. But the captain knows what he's doing."

The crew listened nervously to the sounds of their dying ship as they stood fast, awaiting further orders.

)O(O(

The USS *Young* listed forty-five degrees to starboard as the men scrambled through their slow motion capsize. Sailors struggled for handholds in the quarters below and on the deck above. Topside teams attempted to release the Carley rafts and lifeboats, but found it impossible with the tilt of the deck.

"It's no use, sir," a young sailor said. "Those won't be coming with us."

A lieutenant relayed the news to Captain Calhoun as he clung to a port rail to keep from sliding down the deck into the churning ocean below.

"The lifeboats are no go, Captain. We're listing too fast."

"Then we stay with the ship," Calhoun replied. "Everybody climbs to the port side and follow the hull as she capsizes. Are we clear below?"

"Not yet, sir. Nearly twenty from the engine crew yet to report."

XXX

Below. Below. Water and fuel oil rushed into the *Young's* engine room as the crew raced to climb the ladders. A sudden shift sent the ship and the room to its side and the men fell hard. Heads hit instrument panels. Bones broke. The water followed the sailors, its cold weight knocking them back, pinning them to the bulkhead. It was already waist deep. Able men raised up the injured and looked for an exit, counting their last precious seconds, searching for their chance. The port hatch hung high out of reach above; the starboard was lost to the black below. Some dove, pulling themselves forward hand over hand against the current, only to float up again, desperate for breath as they slipped across the rapidly rising surface like leaves riding a stream. Then the water began to rush in from overhead as well in an unswimmable fall of breath-crushing force. And then the lights went out.

〉〇〈〇〈

The *Young* lay on its side with nearly eighty men struggling to help one another from the deck to the hull. They secured lines where they could, smashing porthole windows for handholds. In the distance, spotlights shone and sirens sounded from the *Delphy*, the *Woodbury*, the *Nicholas*, and the *Lee*, desperate signals for the rest of the squadron. And then, coming on fast, there was the USS *Farragut* racing dead straight toward the wreck of the *Young*.

〉〇〈〇〈

A *Farragut* lieutenant, as yet oblivious to the calamity, peered forward into the fog until he saw—what?

"Christ, hard to port! Full stern!"

The helmsman at the wheel turned hard. Another lieutenant yanked the EOT handle. The ship turned sharply to port and began to slow with the spin of its propellers reversed against forward momentum.

〢〢〢

The USS *Fuller* appeared from the fog just behind the *Farragut*. The *Fuller* turned hard to starboard, grazing the *Farragut's* propellers and stern and tearing a gash in its own hull. Continuing forward, the *Fuller* slammed the shoals of the same small, steep island as the *Woodbury*, coming to rest beside it.

〢〢〢

Captain Calhoun helped pull the last few crew over the rail from the deck onto the hull. He stood to survey the situation—all these men struggling for purchase on an unstable, sinking ship. He scanned the chopping sea with binoculars as his second in command, Lieutenant Herzinger, beside him did the same.

"It looks like maybe three hundred yards ahead," Herzinger said, estimating the distance to shore.

"It's a suicide swim."

The water was black and turbulent. Heavy waves broke over a jagged shoreline. But stepping forth from the crowd of men huddled behind them, Chief Boatswain's Mate Arthur Peterson volunteered without hesitation.

"I'll do it, sir."

"Do what, sailor? Even if you get to shore with a line, how do we get the rest of these men through that reef?"

And then the uss *Chauncey* raced past at full speed, still twenty knots, oblivious to the carnage around it, straight past the *Young* and hard into the rocks at shore.

"That'll cut the distance, Captain," Peterson replied, "and give us a nice bridge to boot."

He pulled off his shirt and shoes, ready for the swim.

XXX

On the creaking *Delphy,* Lattimore and Tipsword made their way atop the windy bridge to reconnect the radio to the fallen antennae tower.

"Jesus," Tipsword said. "Look at that. Jesus."

From their high view and through a momentary break in the fog they could see the confusion below on the deck of the *Delphy.* They also saw the *Lee* and the *Nicholas* stranded to shore off their port, the *Chauncey* on rocks ahead of their starboard bow, the *Young* capsized and swarming with sailors to their starboard, the stranded *Woodbury* and *Fuller* skerry-wedged several hundred yards to sea, the *Farragut*, wounded but worthy, backing out of danger, and farther astern the running lights of six more ships fast headed their way. It had been less than a handful of minutes since they first struck land.

Lattimore took the radio and made the call as Tipsword struggled to reconnect the wiring.

"All ships DesRon 11. *Delphy* aground. Repeat, *Delphy* and others aground. Suggest immediate course correction south or west. Repeat, slow and make immediate course correction south or west."

And then with a great crack below, something in the ship's structure snapped, almost throwing the men from atop the bridge. The antennae tower finished its collapse, taking their radio—and almost the lieutenants with it—to the deck far below.

Warning bells sounded and the alert went out: All hands on deck.

In fast but orderly columns, sailors emerged and took their emergency stations. They stumbled as the ship jerked beneath them, as the deck buckled and folded aft of the midship deckhouse with a great screech, as the hull broke open wide.

NIGHT IN THE WATER

Haines stopped mid-shuffle as his cell jerked with this latest rending of the ship. Several sailors ran past up the passageway.

"Did I miss something?" Haines called out.

An apprentice seaman stopped, surprised to see someone in the brig.

"Haines. We'll get you out of there. I'll find someone."

And the man ran on.

Haines looked down the now tilted passageway and saw it filling with water below. He finished his shuffle, gathered the deck, and turned the top card. It was the ace of spades—the death card. Whether it came up by chance or through his own sleight of hand even Haines did not know.

"Come back to me, Emmett," Ruby said.

I will.

)O(O(

Arthur Peterson stepped shoeless across the bow of the capsized USS *Young*. The rivets on the cold steel hull hurt the soles of his feet at first, but as the waves sloshed over the hull and he moved deeper, first to his ankles and then his knees and hips, he grew numb to the pain. His concern at that point was simply not to fall, to keep himself upright as he approached the cutting edge of the bow, and to be aware as he reached it so as not to misjudge his final steps. He clung tight with both hands to the line that his shipmates fed to him as the distance between them increased. At last he found the edge. He was more than waist deep now. With a final determined breath he dove forward, losing himself in the black. He came up for another deep, salty breath, treading water. He turned back to Captain Calhoun and the lieutenant.

"Make us proud, sailor."

Shifting the line to one hand, he waved at the men then turned and began to breaststroke away. The water was incredibly cold—more so than he had expected—but stripped down to his undergarments he floated well enough and for now at least there was no breaking surf to worry his progress.

His biggest trouble, unexpected and immediately apparent, was the dark. The fog was thick enough that there were no stars, no moon above to guide his way. And low to the water's surface there was no sign of the *Chauncey* ahead. Turning back and pausing, he could make out the sound of voices from the *Young*, but already he had lost sight of it. Only as he crested each swell could he imagine the indistinct line of the destroyer on its side, the crew clinging to its surface like ants on a floating log.

There was nothing to do but pick a direction and swim.

"Give him a light," someone shouted. "Not on him. A target."

And then a beam crossed the water to his left—he had been headed for the deep—and he corrected course.

"How long do you think we've got, Captain?"

"Not long. But if that young man is as lucky as he is brave, maybe long enough."

Arthur Peterson redoubled his efforts against the sea.

XOXOX

Eugene Dooman sat in Captain Watson's cabin listening to the muffled chaos and sirens. He heard the voices through the walls.

"She's lost. We're losing fuel oil at the breach."

"God help us if she sparks."

"They'll roll some heads for this."

Dooman cautiously opened the cabin door and looked into the abandoned passageway. He looked back at the cabin, at the playing cards and the money scattered from desk to floor, and at the empty glasses broken in the sink. Captain Watson's officer's sword and a framed picture of Mrs. Watson were fixed to one wall.

Dooman retrieved both of those, leaving the cards and the money behind.

He exited the cabin then walked down the short passageway, opened another hatch, and stepped outside into disorder and confusion—at least it seemed like that to Dooman, but in truth the wet deck played host to a lot of well trained men carrying out their well rehearsed emergency response.

Chief Quartermaster Cummings spotted him standing there and ushered him out of the way.

"Mr. Dooman, I was just coming to find you."

"What happened?"

"It seems we've discovered an island that isn't on the charts. That's the only possible explanation for a cockup of this magnitude, at least until the Navy tells us otherwise."

Dooman nodded, not knowing what else to say.

"Let's see about getting you off this wreck, shall we?"

Cummings began to lead Dooman forward but the hurried approach of an apprentice seaman interrupted his task.

"Sir," the man said. "It's Haines. He's still in the brig."

"Goddammit." This was a new priority. "Come with me, sailor. Mr. Dooman, you wait here."

Cummings and the sailor rushed off as fast as they could toward the aft deck. The commotion gave pause to a nearby group of sailors—Grady, Forsythe, and

Pearson. Pearson called out to the former two: "It's Emmett. He's still in the brig."

All three dropped their duties and ran off to follow Cummings.

Dooman stood dumbfounded, as lost and out of place and in the way as ever.

Then he, too, hurried after Cummings and the others.

)O(O(

Peterson swam. Somewhere behind him, a world away even if only a stone's throw, men stood on the rocking hull of the *Young* and fed out the line, inches at a time. He never felt it tighten but he could feel its drag. He had lost the light that guided him and now he swam blind, numb to the cold and his tongue numb from salt. The dark water rose and fell. He stopped to tread in place and take stock. He choked a bit on a mouthful of rogue ocean. There was no *Chauncey* ahead, no *Young* behind, only him alone and the careless sea and the fog that swallowed all sound—or maybe his ears had gone numb as well. And then a flicker of light in the distance, fuzzy through the moist air. Not the *Chauncey*, no, not his destination. It was the light from the *Young*, pushing him away, urging him on. He turned from it and swam.

)O(O(

The *Delphy* lay broken in two pieces with its bow balanced on the shore reef at the base of a sheer cliff and the aft of its midsection angled under the water. Further back, the stern rose up again, rocking with the waves that alternately pushed it and pulled it from and toward the deep. Both sections of the ship swayed in time with the billowing sea.

Cummings and the apprentice made their way back from the bow and entered the midship deckhouse, abandoned now. Pearson, Grady, and Forsythe entered just behind them. They dropped down an awkwardly angled ladder and found the water already at their shins. The depth increased as the passageway sloped down. The rocking amplified the sea splash confined within the narrow corridor.

"Emmett, you there?" Forsythe called out, stepping past the quartermaster and the others.

His words met only the muffled echo of the water. The damaged ship creaked all around them as they pushed forward, flashlights pointing the way. The passage was flooded to the ceiling before they reached the cell.

"Oh no," Grady said.

"I'm going in." That was Pearson. He took the cell key from Cummings and dove beneath the surface. It was dark down there, barely illuminated by the light beams refracted through the water. He swam down until he found a handhold on a cell bar, then pulled himself deeper to the door. He fumbled with the key toward the lock, but there was already something there, something jamming the keyhole—two stick-like objects—and the door began to swing open.

Pearson swam back to the surface and rejoined his shipmates, replenishing his lungs with a deep breath of damp air. He hadn't thought about the cold, but it hit him now.

"Emmett?" Grady asked.

Pearson could only shake his head: no. They were crestfallen at the news, but Pearson handed to Grady the items he had pulled from the lock. Forsythe shined a light as Grady unrolled them, revealing two halves of a playing card that had been torn neatly lengthwise and rolled to form a pair of lock picks. It was, or had been, the ace of spades.

"Fuckin' Emmett," Pearson said, cracking his first smile in a long time.

XOXOX

Dooman waited outside the deckhouse for Cummings and the others. The ship seemed abandoned, everyone else having moved to higher ground at the bow. He looked down at the surface of the water where it met the deck—it appeared to be rising, or more likely the ship was continuing to sink—and then across the expanse to the broken stern where it rose again.

Between the two halves, waves splashed across submerged deck-mounted torpedo tubes and damaged lifeboats. It seemed an impassable barrier, and so Dooman was surprised to spot a lone figure on the abandoned stern: a sailor working by himself to lower a raft and drag it down the sloping deck. It was Haines. The two men made eye contact, then Haines casually saluted Dooman. It did not feel like a mocking salute, merely an acknowledgment of the impossible distance between two men.

Cummings and the others climbed out of the deckhouse. Pearson stood dripping wet and shivering.

"Mr. Dooman, you've joined us," the quartermaster said. "That's probably for the best. Let's see if we can get you into one of these boats." He pointed out a raft on the deckhouse. "You four, launch this raft and escort Mr. Dooman to shore. The rest of the crew will be departing via the bow, but that's a lot to ask of a civilian."

The men went to work following Cummings' order as Cummings returned to the bow. They lowered the raft down the side, that seeming to be a safer approach than moving down the deck through the mess of loose torpedo tubes and collapsing cranes.

Dooman looked back for Haines but the man and his raft were gone.

⅏⅏

The water had begun to take its toll on Peterson as he swam almost aimlessly now, just trying to keep moving. He shivered from the cold and his breathing came slow and shallow. His pulse, had he bothered to take it, had weakened. He was becoming more and more tired by the minute, and for longer and longer stretches he had begun to forget where he was and what he was doing. These were all signs of the hypothermia creeping in as the cold ocean pulled the heat from his body. The size of the seas had begun to increase as well, and an unexpected wave lifted him up and tumbled him perilously close to a reef. He could not see it, but first one arm then the other and a knee made contact as he spun. Somehow he swam clear, or more likely was pulled clear by a momentary mercy of the sea. He saw a bright light cutting the night overhead but wasn't sure if this was real or just a figment of his fading mind.

"Hey, help," he called out weakly. He could barely hear himself above the soft crackling of the salt foam. He treaded water and remembered to check that he still had the line. He did. The light rotated from side to side as it scanned the fog. Peterson swam toward it like a moth drawn to flame.

At last the water lit up around him and excited voices called from above.

"In the water. Man overboard. Man overboard."

A life preserver splashed down beside him and he wrapped an arm through it. It was almost enough excuse to pass into sleep, to let the cold take him away. And then came the lines and ladders and arms that lifted him upward in a dream and somehow he found himself standing in his underwear, dripping, shivering uncontrollably onto the crowded deck of the *Chauncey*. He somehow found the strength to salute the officer standing before him.

"Arthur Peterson," he said, the words barely escaping his throat through an uncontrolled stutter and clatter of teeth. "Chief Boatswain's Mate, uss *Young*."

"Welcome to the *Chauncey*, Mr. Peterson. How can we help?"

Peterson handed off his line to a nearby sailor as others wrapped him in rough wool blankets. He collapsed into their arms.

XXX

Lieutenant Blodgett looked out from the bridge of the *Delphy* to the bow below where a breeches buoy of lines, pulleys, and a life preserver seat had been rigged up to transport men from ship to shore. One after another, sailors rode the buoy down the line as they abandoned ship. The perilous trip over rocks and crashing tide was made more difficult by the ship's rocking, which alternately slackened the lines then pulled them taut.

Blodgett studied his reflection in the glass. The bandage covering the gash in his forehead was stained with blood.

"Captain, it's time," he said.

There came no reply from Captain Watson.

"We're abandoning ship now, sir. The men could use your support."

"There's nothing more for us on the bridge, Captain," Hunter chimed in. "There's nothing we can do from here."

On the beach below, where the line from the *Delphy* was tied off at the rocks, sailors drenched by sea spray and waves worked together to pull the line taut when it slackened. Some of the sailors departing the ship had a more difficult time than others as they were almost tossed from their seat by the jerking of the line. Many were only half dressed and a number of them wore no shoes. Sharp rocks cut their bare, numb feet as they reached land. Some of the earlier arrivals to shore scoured the sand for driftwood. They struggled with cold, numb fingers to start a fire with a match. They stood close to the flames, rubbing their hands.

"Robinson Crusoe never had it so good."

"I wonder where we are."

"I'm just happy to be safe on land. There'll be rescue on the way soon enough."

The men were distracted by desperate shouts from the sailors manning the line.

"Pull! Pull! Bring it tight!"

The men on the line tried to pull back as an unexpectedly deep list of the ship lowered it much further than usual, dipping a dangling sailor near to the ocean's surface. Then the ship rose fast again, yanking the lines once more. The sailor in the breeches buoy rose high and hard. The line at the rocks snapped free of its mooring and from the hands of the sailors, and the man on the line screamed as he was tossed into the air and then fell, limbs flailing, with a thick smack onto the rocks below. The next wave took his body and the buoy seat out to sea.

A sailor crossed himself.

"I couldn't see who that was."

"It was a sailor. It was all of us."

XXXX

After helping lower the Carley raft down the side of the *Delphy*, the apprentice sailor was the first to board. He climbed down a makeshift rope ladder, a bit too short to reach, then dropped the rest of the way. Once aboard, he tried to stabilize the craft for the others as they attempted to join him. It was not an easy job. The raft rocked with the sea, shifting and tilting toward the ship and then away with the whims of the clutching tide. The apprentice held his arms upstretched toward the next in line, the civilian Dooman, while Grady and Forsythe and Pearson waited their turn at the rail above, encouraging the man to make use of the rope ladder from which he dangled.

Dooman held the captain's sword in one hand. The framed picture, buttoned tight beneath the fold of his coat, pressed against his chest. But it was the raft below, far below, its position shifting unpredictably second by second, that drew his attention. He heard the muffled clap of waves against the boards as the sea rose with violence to lift the target, only to collapse and drop away again. He felt the spray on his exposed face and ungloved hands, which refused to unclasp themselves from the ladder. The hands themselves had begun to lose feeling in the cold, and Dooman was no longer sure he could unbend the fingers if he tried.

"I can't do it," he called out to the sailor below.

"Sure you can, Mr. Dooman. You just have to time your jump. I'll catch you." The sailor spread his arms out in a welcoming gesture, one hand still holding the line that connected the raft to the ship. "Although you might want to hand me your sword first. Nobody wants to get stabbed."

Dooman looked down and considered, still immobile.
"Mr. Dooman, come back up." It was Pearson. "I'll board first, then we'll have two of us below to get you into the raft. You'll see how easy it is."

Relieved but humiliated, Dooman climbed back up the ladder and over the rail, onto the ship again. Pearson took his place.

"Careful, Jack. There's a lot of oil splashing around down here."

"I can smell it," Pearson replied. "It's everywhere."

He swayed in the air above the roiling target as he lowered himself toward the raft. It wasn't a huge drop, but in the darkness and numbing cold it was far enough. He waited until the timing was right, then he let go. But as his feet hit the raft's float, slick with fuel oil, they slid out from under him. He fell half in the raft and half out, his head bouncing off the raft floor. The impact combined with the rising swell tossed him up and out, pinning him between the raft and the ship. His face hit the hull hard, shattering his glasses and driving broken shards into his eyes. He fell back into the water, one leg bent at an unnatural angle as the raft continued to batter him against the ship. Dooman watched it all in horror as the others shouted: "Jack! Jack!"

The apprentice sailor in the raft reached out for him but Pearson slipped his grasp and sank beneath the surface.

"Where is he? Where is he? Do you see him?"

But Pearson did not rise.

⚬⚬⚬

Off the stern of the *Delphy* another raft made its way toward shore with a single sailor paddling onboard: Emmett Haines. He heard the panicked shouts from the ship.

"Jack! Jack! Pearson!"

Haines turned back to look. Through the fog he could not see the sailors. He could barely see the damaged stern rising up from the water, stilled propellers exposed—and something floating beneath them. A body?

"Jack?" Haines said. His voice was no more than a whisper. He knew the answer. He knew there would be no reply. He knew what he had to do. There was no need to think twice, not even an urge to do so.

It was too far to paddle back quickly in the ungainly raft, and so he kicked off his shoes and dove beneath the waves and swam.

⚬⚬⚬

Captain Calhoun and Lieutenant Herzinger stood on the hull of the overturned *Young*, their shoes and pants drenched by the wash and spray tugging at their feet. Four score sailors stood helpless behind them, spread out along the hull with nothing to do but hug themselves for warmth and stare into the distance at the taut line Peterson had carried into the fog. Taut was a good sign. It meant he was out there somewhere. He hadn't lost it. Whether he had reached his goal they had no way of knowing—until a dark shape slowly materialized on the water, and another and another behind it— lifeboats powered by lone sailors pulling on the line.

"Permission to come aboard, Captain?" the first called out, only half in jest.

"Permission granted, sailor," Calhoun replied. "Welcome to the uss *Young*."

The stranded sailors began to cheer.

)O(O(

The abandonment of the *Delphy* continued apace. Without the buoy seat, sailors were forced to travel monkey style, hand over hand, dangling from the line spun from their dying ship to its tenuous attachment point at the rocks on shore. Much of the crew had already made their way to safety, the process having been well drilled and efficiently carried out, aside from the one unfortunate accident.

Lieutenant Commander Hunter and Lieutenant Blodgett observed the evacuation along with Captain Watson, who by now was at least engaged enough to gasp with the others as a sailor almost lost his grip on the line. The man recovered, though, and made his way to the rocks, where he was greeted warmly. Bonfires now dotted the beach, with small groups of sailors huddled around to regain the feeling in their frozen hands.

And now it was time for Sofronio Dalida, the captain's cook, to take his turn. But it was not so easy.

"No. No, I can't do it," he said.

"You can, Dalida," a sailor encouraged. "It's easy."

"I'm a cook. I learn to peel potatoes, not swing like a monkey."

Watson at last recovered the courage to lead. He placed a hand on Dalida's shoulder. "Sofronio, you can do this. I promise you."

"Captain?"

"You have my word. You'll be safe. Just put one hand in front of the other and you'll be on the beach before you know it."

Dalida nodded. He trusted his captain. He climbed over the rail and lowered himself onto the line.

"Good man, Sofronio. See how easy it is?"

Captain Watson's return to form cheered the men, who cheered Dalida.

"You can do it, Dalida," a sailor said. "The hard part's over."

But Dalida still had a ways to go and each change of grip was a fearful challenge. And then halfway across, another lurch of the ship caught the men at the line below off guard. Like the earlier sailor, Dalida was jerked from the line. He fell to the rocks, his legs snapping as they hit. In agony he cried for help from the wash of sea and stone until the waves stole him away.

This was all too much for Captain Watson.

XOXOX

Dalida's screams could barely be heard in the distance, but even so Grady and Forsythe were too busy with shouts of their own to notice.

"Jack! Jack! Where is he?"

Dooman looked on horrified as the apprentice sailor called up from the raft. "I don't see him. Has he come up? Pearson! Pearson!"

XOXOX

Haines swam behind the stern, chasing after the body in the current. Closer now, he could see the sheen of oil on the surface of the water ahead. He dove under it and swam, pulling with all his might through the breathless dark. He rose gasping into a calm eddy behind the stern. The water here was clear of oil. Pearson's body floated nearby.

"Jack," Haines called out. "Jack."

He swam closer and lifted Pearson's head above water, getting his first look at the man's face—a bloody mess with broken nose and deep cuts to the eyes. He still wore the twisted mess of his shattered eyeglasses.

Haines took hold of Pearson and sidestroked around to the starboard side of the ship. This more difficult approach, with the destroyer listing away and the waves breaking into the open hull, was at least clear of oil in the water.

"Grady!" he shouted. "Forsythe!" But there came no reply.

He made for the broken aft deck but he couldn't overcome the power of the current that pushed him toward the main ship. The jagged edges of the deck rose and fell with the chop as swamped, loose lifeboats pounded the fixtures. And then he was in it, twisting and tumbling, one arm fast around Pearson, the other flailing for control. The water slammed them against the torpedo tubes, against the deck, against a rail, against a lifeboat—and then the lifeboat slipped back toward them and caught Haines' left hand between its outer rail and one of the fixed torpedo tubes. He heard the crush of bones over the roar of the tide racing out.

XOXOX

Haines' agonized howl reached Grady and Forsythe, who ran aft to find him, climbing down then up the listing deck. Dooman followed. They arrived just in time to see Haines struggling to his feet, limping for higher ground through a departing wave, dragging Pearson with one arm.

"Jack. Emmett, thank God. Oh, Jesus, Jack."

The men laid Pearson out on deck but they found no breath in him. His face was streaked with blood and oil, his legs shattered. Haines collapsed beside him, holding his own arm at the wrist just short of the mangled left hand.

Grady and Forsythe attempted to revive Pearson and at last he coughed, spitting up a lungful of oily seawater. But as soon as he became conscious he began to thrash about and scream. They struggled to keep him still.

"Emmett, help," Forsythe begged. But then he looked back to Emmett and saw his hand. "Christ, Em." He turned to Dooman. "You. Get the medic. Now."

Dooman had merely watched up to this point, uselessly stunned, but he came to life at the order. He dropped the sword and ran back up the ship.

"Medic, medic," he shouted. "Where's the medic? We need a doctor."

Even at the bow he could still hear Pearson's screams. The screams carried all the way to the beach, where sailors shuddered and crossed themselves, and to the hull of the *Young*, mostly empty now save for Calhoun and a few others loading the last of the rescue boats.

"God protect the souls of all who perished here tonight," Calhoun said.

Even farther out to sea, to where the *Woodbury* and the *Fuller* jammed fast to the outcrop of rocks, one ship listing starboard and the other to port, sailors heard the screams. Some had made it into lifeboats of their own while others had scrambled from the derelict hulks onto the rocks themselves, where they huddled together against the cold fog and sea spray and prayed for rescue before the turn of the tide. They heard Pearson's screams and grew colder than ever before.

"Doctor," Dooman called out again. "We need a doctor."

"What now?" replied the quartermaster. "I thought you were off the ship, Mr. Dooman." He stood among the last few men on board, including Watson, Blodgett, Hunter, and the pharmacist's mate.

"Two men badly injured," Dooman said in a rush. "We need a doctor."

"You'll have to settle for me," said the pharmacist's mate, picking up his aid kit.

And now Dooman relaxed a bit, just enough to notice his friend. "Ed. Captain. Ed, I have your—" But Dooman trailed off as Captain Watson never acknowledged him, never made eye contact, just stood there lost in his own head.

"Lead the way, Mr. Dooman," commanded Cummings.

Dooman tried again. "Ed?" But there was nothing.

Another scream from down ship brought him back to priorities at hand. He led the pharmacist's mate and Cummings away. When they reached the struggling sailors they found Grady and Forsythe still attempting to restrain the thrashing Pearson.

"Jack, stay calm. Stay calm. Help is on the way."

"We'll get you off this ship. We'll get you safe and warm."

He gave no sign that he heard them as he flailed blindly, cuffing them, flopping about with his broken legs dangling like a rag doll's.

Haines leaned back against the deckhouse, gently cradling his crushed, rapidly swelling hand.

"Is this my fault?"

He said it to no one in particular and the others were so busy with Pearson that they didn't hear. Haines rejoined them and with his good hand he stroked Pearson's head, trying to calm him.

"Is this my fault?"

"Don't say that, Em," said Grady.

"I wasn't there. I should have been there."

At the touch of Haines' hand on his forehead, Pearson relaxed a bit and stopped fighting. Grady and Forsythe loosened their grip on his arms.

"It was an accident. You weren't steering the course."

"You were looking for me. That's what brought you back."

He continued to stroke Pearson's head. Pearson seemed to recognize his friends despite his blood-stained eyes. He lifted a hand and Grady took it.

"There you go, Jack. Here I am. Here we are."

"Holy Christ," Cummings said, kneeling beside Pearson and getting his first look at the injuries.

"He lost his footing boarding the raft," Forsythe explained. "Crushed against the hull. Eyeglasses shattered. Swallowed a lungful of oil. Haines fished him out and we got him breathing again."

"Brutal mercies," said the pharmacist's mate, who could see at a glance where this was headed. He knelt to examine the injuries but as soon as he touched Pearson the screams began again. Pearson lunged and thrashed about with both arms so that the men had to retreat.

"Hold him down. Hold him down," Cummings commanded.

It wasn't easy. Haines was no help with just one hand and Dooman still stood back, unsure what use he could be. The other four were unable to control the raging, injured Pearson.

All around them the ship moaned and popped as it continued to break apart at the seams. It lurched beneath their feet and the men stumbled.

"Bring us a line," Cummings said to Haines. "We'll tie him down and lower him to the raft."

Pearson screamed again: "No, no, no."

With his good arm Haines lugged a heavy line to Cummings. As he handed it over, the pharmacist's mate saw the damage to his hand.

"That doesn't look good, sailor."

"As long as I have my hands …"

The pharmacist's mate left Pearson to the others and took his kit to Haines. He examined the injury.

"You'll need a real doctor. You'll need more than I can give you tonight." Haines steeled himself as the man manipulated his wrist and fingers and felt the bones beneath the skin. He cleaned and dressed the wound, wrapping it in heavy bandages. "You'll be wanting morphine."

Haines shook him off and directed him back to Pearson, who could not be controlled, who continued to scream and thrash.

"Dammit, man, we're trying to help." Cummings was losing patience. "Tie him to the ship, then. We'll have to leave him here and come back when he's calmed."

Haines watched with concern as they looped the line around Pearson's chest and fixed the other end to the deckhouse. The disintegration of the *Delphy* seemed to be accelerating.

At this point Dooman finally snapped out of his stunned reverie. "Mr. Haines," he began. "I'm so sorry about your friend. I'm so sorry about your ship." He picked up the sword that he had left behind earlier. "I saved this for your captain. He'll be wanting it later but he's too busy now to retrieve it himself."

Haines had no interest in this—no interest in Dooman, in the ship, in the sword, in the captain. His friend was dying.

"Oh, and your money," Dooman continued, oblivious. "I left it in Captain Watson's cabin. I've come to realize that it must have been yours all along. You're an honorable man, Mr. Haines, I can see that now. But it's not too late. We can still get it back for you, I think. I'll put in a good word."

With that, Haines had had enough.

"Damn the money. Damn the money and damn you, Mr. Dooman."

"Haines, calm yourself," said Cummings.

"To hell with you and your goddamn captain and this whole goddamn ship."

It was as if his curse were enough to bring down the ship itself. Behind them the rigging for a sailing launch crane snapped. The stern of the launch hammered the deck as the crane leaned into a high spotlight platform, beginning a slow collapse for both.

"This isn't the time or the place, Haines, whatever you're on about."

But Haines stood, ignoring Cummings and the danger of the unstable rigging. He marched to Pearson, who screamed and thrashed against the others. Once again he sat beside Pearson and stroked his head.

"Leave us," he said. Nobody moved, so he said it again—shouting this time. "Just leave us. Get off this goddamn boat and leave us in peace."

Everybody backed off except for the pharmacist's mate, who slipped Haines a packet of morphine.

"Your friend. This will help."

Haines nodded his thanks then looked to Grady, who stood by reluctant to retreat any farther.

"It's okay, Earl. It's my watch. You don't need to see this."

Then the crane crashed onto the deck between them in a heap of twisted metal and cables. Haines looked only at Pearson as the others hurried to safety.

XXX

The beach is lined with bonfires and sailors. Grady, Forsythe, Cummings, Dooman, the pharmacist's mate, and the apprentice paddle the raft toward shore. The pharmacist's mate looks back to see the wreck of the *Delphy* shrouded in fog, disappearing from sight.

Pearson's screams fly low across the water. They travel forward across the bow and to shore, where Captain Watson stands alone on the rocks, staring back at his ship, ignoring the spray of waves against his uniform. Can he even hear the screams? Or are the screams the only thing he hears?

The hull of the *Young* is empty now, the waves gently washing across it, floating the tied handholds left behind by the men.

Pearson's screams echo in the distance.

The listing *Woodbury* and *Fuller* sway with the waves. Nearly eighty sailors sit stranded upon the rocks, shivering cold and desperate in the fog and shivering again at the lonely screams from the unseen *Delphy*.

"Let's sing him to sleep, boys," says one old salt. He begins to sing an old sea song, soon joined by the others for the chorus, their voices hesitant and warbling with the cold at first but then gaining force:

Safe and sound at home again,
Let the waters roar, Jack.
Safe and sound at home again,
Let the waters roar, Jack.
Long we've tossed on the rolling main,
Now we're safe ashore, Jack.

Don't forget your old shipmate,
Faldee raldee raldee raldee rye-eye-doe.

Pearson screams and thrashes as Haines tries to calm him.

"There, Jack. There. Easy, boy."

Pearson is in agony. The pain is too great. He's dying and it's taking too long. But he relaxes to another verse and a chorus from the *Woodbury* sailors, perched like sirens on their sea-shot crag.

Since we sailed from Plymouth Sound,
Four years gone or nigh, Jack.
Was there ever chummies now,
Such as you or I, Jack?

Haines holds Pearson propped in his lap, his injured hand on Pearson's chest and his good hand stroking his hair.

"Easy, Jack. Not much longer."

He fumbles with the morphine, trying to prep the needle with his good hand.

We have worked the self-same gun,
Quarterdeck division.
Sponger I and loader you,
Through the whole commission.

Pearson struggles to speak.

"Em … I'm … Sorry."

"So am I, Jack. So am I."

Pearson's hand reaches for his pocket but the ship jerks and the deck tilts abruptly. Haines tightens his grip to keep Pearson from joining the loose wreckage as it slides into the sea. Pearson cries out in pain again.

Sailors at the bonfires listen to the screams from the *Delphy*, but they also faintly hear the song drifting out from the night.

Oftentimes have we laid out,
Toil nor danger fearing,
Tugging at the flapping sail,
To the weather earring.

One by one the sailors leave their bonfires and walk to the water's edge, mournful ghosts in the fog. They join with the chorus.

Long we've tossed on the rolling main,
Now we're safe ashore, Jack.
Don't forget your old shipmate,
Faldee raldee raldee raldee rye-eye-doe.

Pearson screams. Haines gets the morphine right.

"Easy now. This will help."

He injects Pearson, who relaxes into his arms.

When the middle watch was on,
And the time went slow, boy,
Who would choose a rousing stave,
Who like Jack or Joe, boy?

The distant chorus repeats from shore and sea as Pearson manages his final words in his morphine haze.

"Em? Ma?"

"Right here, Jackie. Good boy."

"Let … me … go."

Haines leans forward and kisses Pearson good night. He does not fight the tears as he pulls the line from around Pearson's chest and releases his hold. Pearson's last move is to pull the wallet from his pocket and pass it to Haines—and then he slides down the deck into the water. The waves pull him under.

There she swings, an empty hulk,
Not a soul below now.
Number seven starboard mess,
Misses Jack and Joe now.

Dooman stands on shore near the empty raft, sword in hand, alone. He stares back out to the foggy sea. The night is alive with the sound of sailors singing the song's chorus.

But the best of friends must part,
Fair or foul the weather.
Hand your flipper for a shake,
Now a drink together.

Haines sits alone, watching the spot where Pearson went under, still feeling him beneath the surface, floating as his lungs fill with brine, suspended for all time as the distant chorus repeats:

Oh long we've tossed on the rolling main,
Now we're safe ashore, Jack.
Don't forget your old shipmate,
Faldee raldee raldee raldee rye-eye-doe.

And now there is silence. Nothing but the sounds of the night ocean and the dying ship scraping the ancient floor.

Haines opens the wallet and looks inside: a train ticket, a thick stack of cash, a letter of credit in the name of Eugene Dooman—cursed treasure, all of it. He closes the wallet, taking nothing from it, and hurls it into the sea.

And then Haines, too, loosens his hold and slides into the water below. Alone in her bed, her eyes wide in the dark, Ruby's heart races. She knows.

AFTERMATH

In the morning the papers will report the news:

> "Two dozen sailors are drowned and injured. Seven
> destroyers of the Pacific fleet are held fast on the
> bar off Santo Miguello light."

But that night the sailors stood on the beach or sat on
their rock perches, their song finished, only listening.
The screams from the *Delphy* ended, the injured man
slept at last. It came as a relief.

> "These are the consequences of the Navy's major
> marine disaster in Pacific waters."

And then an even greater relief: a long, loud train
whistle not far away. The men turned their backs to the
sea and looked to the bluffs rising up from the beach.

> "The injured are being nursed at a hospital here. A
> trainload of survivors is headed for San Diego."

Lights shone down upon them from the clifftops,
first one or two, then more and more as people arrived

on foot and in automobiles. They climbed down the cliffs on unseen pathways, their arms loaded with boxes. These Good Samaritans moved among them, from bonfire to bonfire, passing out the things the sailors needed most: warm blankets and dry clothing and jackets and food. They laughed and hugged the sailors and the sailors laughed and all were overjoyed to see one another.

※※※

Ruby bought a paper from a sidewalk stand. The headlines shouted the news:

> "Destroyer Squadron on California Rocks; Seven
> Warships Piled Up on Bar Off Santo Miguello Light;
> Navy's Greatest Disaster On Coast; Theory
> Expressed by Naval Officials that Tidal Wave or
> Seismic Disturbance Caused Wrecks."

She opened the paper to another related story on the inside pages:

> "Ghastly Tragedy Enacted Aboard Destroyer *Delphy*;
> Legs Broken, Blinded By Oil Fumes, Seaman Perishes Despite Heroic Efforts of Comrades."

She read the words aloud:

"September 8, 1923. A tragedy within a tragedy was enacted aboard the destroyer *Delphy*, which went ashore 75 miles north of Santa Barbara Saturday night with six other destroyers of the battle fleet. This tragedy resulted in the death of Seaman Pearson, whose given name and home naval officers at the scene of the wreck were unable to give …"

〤〤〤

By morning most of the fires had burned down to the embers, but sailors still stood around them warming their hands. There was coffee and cooked breakfast: eggs and bacon and toast. A tent had been erected for civilian doctors to attend the wounded.

Dooman walked near the water, still carrying Captain Watson's sword. He had not slept a wink and he looked all the worse for it. With the fog lifted, the wrecked ships were now in full view on and off shore. The hull of the *Young* was barely visible. On the *Delphy*, the deckhouse to which they had tied the sailor Pearson was now almost fully submerged.

"As the *Delphy* dove her bow first into the rugged rocks near Arguello light, Pearson was thrown down a ladder and both legs were broken."

Dooman stepped over a pile of kelp and then paused. He looked back to see, washed up on the sand, water-drenched and oil-stained, a single playing card.

> "His comrades went to his rescue and succeeded in taking him on deck. There he was blinded by oil from bursting fuel pipes. Nearly crazed by pain and desperation he resisted the efforts of shipmates to rig up a breeches buoy to rescue him."

As Dooman picked up the card he saw more cards scattered ahead. He followed the trail along the high tide line to retrieve them all. He was so focused on the cards that he almost bumped into several sailors performing the grim task of lifting a body from the water.

)O(O(

Ruby skimmed ahead through the article, searching out the news she feared most. She read aloud again:

> "The names of additional drowned and missing sailors, including Pearson's fellow crew members, are as yet unavailable pending review by Naval authorities."

Barely able to hold herself together, Ruby dropped the paper to the ground.

XOXOX

Dooman stopped just short of the dead man being pulled from the surf.

"Pardon me," he said. "Excuse me."

The sailors were not happy to see him here. He was an intruder. This was solemn work with no place for gawkers.

"Is that …"

The cards fell from Dooman's hand as they turned the drowned sailor over to place him on a stretcher. But the face was unfamiliar. Dooman followed the men as they carried the corpse to an open tent where several more victims were laid out.

A group of officers stood outside the tent, among them Blodgett, Cummings, Calhoun, the captains of the *Lee*, *Nicholas*, and *Chauncey*, and Captain Watson.

Dooman listened as Blodgett delivered a report.

"Sirs, the count stands at thirty-four men injured, none of them critically. There's a special train scheduled to carry them to Los Angeles for treatment. All men from the *Woodbury* and the *Fuller* have been transferred by fishing boat to the ships of Division 32 under Captain Roper. They've already resumed course for San Diego."

"And the dead?" asked Captain Calhoun.

"We've recovered six bodies so far, Captain. Two from the *Delphy* and four from the *Young*. Sixteen from the

Young remain unaccounted for, and we have two missing off the *Delphy*."

Captain Watson stood apart from the others. He appeared a broken man as he looked at the bodies laid out inside the tent: four drowned sailors from the engine room of the *Young* along with the two who fell to the rocks from his own ship.

And then there was Dooman. He placed a hand on Captain Watson's shoulder but Watson stood unmoved.

"Ed. Captain. I'm sorry. I saved these for you from your cabin. I knew you'd want them."

Dooman took the framed photo of Watson's wife from his pocket and handed it to the captain along with the sword. Watson stared at the photo as if unable to recognize the woman. He nodded just briefly and put it into his pocket. Then he entered the tent and laid his sword across the body of Sofronio Dalida—the sword that a captain no longer deserved. Without looking back, Watson exited the tent and walked down the beach toward the water, away from the activity on shore.

"Captain," Dooman called after him. "Captain. Ed."

But Captain Watson just kept moving.

"Mr. Dooman. It would be best for Captain Watson—best for everyone, really—if you continued on to Los Angeles now." This was Cummings. "A train is waiting."

He took Dooman by the arm and guided him away from the tent. They passed groups of sailors eating breakfast, packing equipment, and organizing the campsite. Working hard anonymously among them was Arthur Peterson, last night's swimming hero of the *Young*—by day just another sailor happy to pull his weight.

"The missing men from the *Delphy*," Dooman said, stopping to Cummings' annoyance. "The two. Would that be Mr. Haines and his friend?"

"You should forget about last night, Mr. Dooman. Let last night forget about you. No good can come from dwelling on it."

Dooman pulled his arm free of Cummings' hand. "I'm a grown man. I'm perfectly well capable of deciding for myself which thoughts I dwell upon. What happened to Mr. Haines?"

"When does the sea give up her dead, sir? Answer me that, and I'll tell you what happened to your man."

"So he never made it off the ship?"

"He hasn't walked into camp. There's no body found. More than that who can say?"

The two men faced off, staring one another down, until at last the quartermaster ran out of patience.

"Your train, Mr. Dooman."

But as Dooman began to acquiesce, he saw something in the distance—a sailor standing apart, his left hand bandaged. The man seemed to make eye contact with Dooman before turning and stepping inside a tent. As tired as he was, Dooman broke away and sprinted after him as hard as he could across the beach.

"Stop. Hey, stop."

As he reached the tent and stepped inside, though, he found himself alone. The space was empty, no back exit, nothing.

Cummings followed him in.

"Mr. Dooman, I really must insist. You'll feel better with rest."

✕✕✕

The *Daylight Limited*, normally non-stop from San Francisco to Los Angeles, sat with its engine car idling along a sandy, wind-blasted stretch of track. There was no station in sight, just rolling hills empty of all but sagebrush. Healthy sailors helped the last few injured men aboard and a conductor closed the doors.

Eugene Dooman chose a window seat and sat looking out toward the sea beyond the desolate landscape. The car was empty except for a half dozen sailors resting quietly.

The train began to move. Dooman tried to brush sand and salt from his trousers but succeeded only in smearing stained oil. A train porter arrived with a bundle of fresh clothing.

"I can't guarantee the fit, sir, but they're clean. We've got fresh water and extra soap and towels in the lavatory."

Dooman made his way to the toilet where he braced himself against the wall as the room rattled and swayed. He washed his hands and face gently, lathering up with plenty of soap, but nothing wanted to come clean. He began to scrub harder and harder with a towel as if to rub away the skin. He did not realize he was crying until he looked up and saw himself in the mirror.

He paused and then the sobs came full force. He let his head hit the glass, perhaps the only thing still holding him up.

✕✕✕

Grady and Forsythe sat together on the beach, staring out at what was left of the *Delphy* and the wreckage of near half their squadron.

"I saw him last night, you know," Grady said. "After the fires died. Walking along the shoreline like nothing was wrong."

"Jack or Em?"

"Jack's dead."

Forsythe could not disagree.

"He's a magician, Em is," Grady went on. "He's Houdini. He can get out of anything."

"Even the Navy?"

"Even the Navy. He wasn't cut out for this."

Already this graveyard of ships was being colonized by a new crew: gulls and cormorants roosting on foredecks and atop abandoned bridges and gun turrets. The birds settled and rose up and settled again, as if unsure what to think of these colossal intruders in their timeless world.

"Nobody's cut out for this," Forsythe said. "Not that at least. But Emmett was as much a sailor as any of us. Better, even, in the end."

"He was built for bigger things, though, wasn't he? We won't be seeing him again."

It was late in the day already. In a few hours the sun would set, and then the next day it would rise and set again and again and then what would be the point of it all? In the long years to come who would remember Emmett Haines and Jack Pearson and all the rest who perished here and even those who lived?

"Somebody will," Forsythe said. "Somebody has to."

XOXOX

Dooman returned to his seat, composure regained, face freshly scrubbed, his hair damp and matted, combed with nothing but a towel. His new clothes, while not up to his accustomed quality, were fresh and clean.

He sat and closed his eyes. He woke moments or hours later to the sound of shuffling cards.

Haines sat across from him, showered and shaved, dressed in crisp, clean, Navy whites. His left hand was bandaged but functional. He fanned his cards on the seat table, flipped them to reveal a shuffled deck, then flipped them face down again.

"We've been here before," Dooman said.

"Again and again. You make your pick."

Haines tapped the fanned deck.

"That's probably not the best idea," Dooman protested.

"You don't have a choice."

Dooman picked a card and turned it up: the ace of spades.

With his bandaged hand dripping wet, draped in sea-weed, Haines flipped the deck. Every card an ace of spades.

"I never lose," Haines said, bloated and blue, his uniform soaked, torn, and barnacled by the sea. He winked at Dooman, who shook his head rapidly—a reset for his brain—and Haines appeared normal again, clean and dry in his fresh uniform.

"I'm dreaming," Dooman said. "I'm hallucinating."

"You must be very tired after all you've been through."

Haines, or the specter of Haines, ran his monte game now with three cards. He turned them face up to show two black jacks and a red queen. Then he turned them face down and mixed them up again.

"Or perhaps I'm being haunted," Dooman mused.

"It passes the time. It keeps me out of trouble."

Dooman chose one of the cards. Haines flipped it to reveal another ace of spades.

"Bad luck for us," Haines said.

Then he gathered the full deck again and shuffled, holding it up before Dooman and flipping through the cards. It was a classic magician's trick, a force, with all the cards a blur except for the briefest pause on just one, just the one that mattered.

Dooman woke with a start. He was alone but in his mind a voice echoed: "Pick a card. Any card."

He stood and looked back at the train car. Nothing had changed. The same half dozen sailors slept in the same seats, undisturbed. There was no sign of anyone else, not a closing door, not the flutter of a curtain.

He sat again but now there was something new on the seat facing him, something that had not been there before: a playing card, neatly centered on the seat, face down.

He hesitated then reached out to touch it, to turn it over—

The four of clubs.

XXXX

We are bound by time. These things happened as surely as death comes for us all. And yet the echoes fade as minutes turn to years turn to centuries. A wave that means so much to one man falls to a ripple subsumed by the wider ocean. A touch becomes the memory of a touch. A secret kiss between lovers, the highlight of a life, is lost to history. The government demands reports and reports are filed and forgotten. They dynamite storm-tossed wrecks and drag them to deeper waters, out of sight and out of mind. One hundred years later only the hulk of one lone boiler continues to rise up at low tide, rusted and flattened and unrecognizable on a battered reef, home to urchin and starfish and crab.

We read the names and the dates on the weathered memorial but we are bound by time, we to ours and they to theirs. We know an approximation of fates but some secrets will never be revealed—perhaps not until the moment we know our own, perhaps not even then. We can only imagine.

We imagine the old train pulling through unspoiled California countryside, land that remains unspoiled to this day, reaching and crossing a lonely road, coyote and crow the only witness to its passing. As the final car clears the asphalt, all that remains is swirling dust and smoke and a man in ill-fitting civilian clothes, one hand heavily bandaged. The clatter of metal wheels on the tracks recedes and he looks to a simple road sign with two arrows: Los Angeles one way, San Francisco the other.

We imagine the choice is easy.

Ruby sits alone watching a movie she has seen a dozen times. It comes as light comfort now. There is laughter all around her in the audience, but she does all she can to hold back her tears as the actor clings for life to the broken clock high above the busy street, as he will cling endlessly for all time as time runs its never-ending course. Her pained expression softens ever so slightly as a bandaged hand comes to rest on her arm.

The Wreck at Honda Point

The Wreck at Honda Point

Dead Reckoning is a work of fiction based on real events. On the night of September 8, 1923, seven ships of the U.S. Navy's Destroyer Squadron 11, led by Commodore Edward H. Watson on board the flagship USS *Delphy*, bore full speed into a treacherous section of California coastline informally known as Honda Point. Traveling south in single file "follow the leader" formation, the ships were attempting a turn into the Santa Barbara channel in heavy fog. They missed by several miles. One after another, in a span of just minutes, the destroyers jammed themselves to the rugged rocks that would be their fate. It was among the worst peacetime disasters in the Navy's history, and remains to this day the greatest loss in number of ships.

Why did this accident happen? That was the question on everyone's mind in the weeks and months that followed—although due to the initial secrecy of the Navy's inquiry, it seemed at times as if the Navy itself might have been less than eager for the answer.

Theories as to the cause at first centered around atypical currents related to recent seismic activity in Japan, along with perceived unreliability of the relatively new Radio Direction Finder system. Visibility was poor that night, but the ships were more than capable of operating under such conditions. There were rumors of alcohol use by the commodore, but these rumors were never substantiated (or even investigated). Likewise, there was no mention at the inquest of the mysterious guest who visited the bridge of the *Delphy* and spent much of the voyage in conversation with Watson in his quarters. Eugene H. Dooman would remain unnamed in accounts of that day for nearly four decades until finally sharing his version of events in the books *Tragedy at Honda* (Charles A. Lockwood and Hans Christian Adamson, 1960) and *The Last Hours of Seven Four-Stackers* (Charles Hice, 1967).

In the end, it came down to human error. The Radio Direction Finder had provided the *Delphy* with accurate position information, which the ship's navigator chose

The USS *Delphy,* DD-261. The *Delphy* and all other ships involved in the Honda Point disaster were *Clemson*-class destroyers, recognizable by their flush decks and four stacks. An update to the earlier *Wickes* class, they were constructed in abundance in the years following World War I. So many were made, in fact, that the loss of seven ships was no great inconvenience. They were quickly replaced by surplus ships that had previously been built and deactivated without seeing service.

to disregard in favor of his own dead reckoning estimates. These estimates were made based on the speed and direction of the ship since its last known position. And this is where those unusual seas come into play. Ship speed in those days was calculated as a function of propeller speed, but with the ships yawing badly against the current, and with the propellers rising up out of the water with the larger swells, the calculated speed was greater than the actual speed. Over the course of the many hours since their last land sighting earlier that day, that added up to a significant error in the dead reckoning position estimate.

As for the many ships trailing the *Delphy*, their captains were in an awkward position, forced to choose between the conflicting imperatives of following orders or protecting their ships and men. They were ordered to follow the *Delphy*, but their own navigation should have made them aware of the dangers. At the same time, however, they had been ordered not to use the RDF system, which would have given them the more accurate position information they needed, and to instead rely on information provided by the *Delphy*.

Commander Walter G. Roper, in charge of Division 32 and traveling aboard that division's flagship, the *Kennedy*, summed the dilemma during his testimony on the last day of the Court of Inquiry. The *Kennedy* and the other ships of Division 32, in their position at the rear of the column, had managed to avoid the fate of the others.

> **Question:** Had you intended to follow the *Delphy* around a change of course at 9 o'clock on the night of September 8?
>
> **Roper:** I wouldn't have followed the leader around a sixty-five degree turn. I don't believe in following the leader if the leading boy jumps off the barn.

Above, top to bottom: The *Woodbury* (with the *Fuller* barely visible behind), the *Young*, the *Chauncey* (at left) and the *Delphy* broken in two.

Below: The *Nicholas* (at left) and the *S.P. Lee*.

Question: If you had observed the *Delphy* turn to the left, would you have tried to stop her?

Roper: Yes, if I see a man trying to jump out of a fifteen-story window I'd stop him if I could. You can't turn a corner until you reach it, and the *Delphy* had not reached the corner.

Roper's ship had intercepted radio bearings that told him they were closer to shore than expected. "It never occurred to me that other ships did not have the same information I did," he explained. "I expected we were running for Arguello Light to get a definite fix on our position. I thought that was beautiful, superb navigation. You couldn't beat it."

Captain Watson accepted responsibility for the incident, but the Court of Inquiry recommended a trial by general court martial for eleven officers: Watson, Lt. Cmdr. Donald T. Hunter, and Lt. (jg) Lawrence F. Blodgett of the *Delphy;* Capt. Robert Morris, commander of Division 33; Cmdr. William S. Pye of Division 31; Cmdr. Louis P. Davis, captain of the *Woodbury;* Cmdr. William L. Calhoun of the *Young*; Cmdr. William S. Toaz of the *S.P. Lee;* Lt. Cmdr. Walter D. Seed of the *Fuller;* Lt. Cmdr. Herbert O. Roesch of the *Nicholas;* and Lt. Cmdr. Richard H. Booth of the *Chauncey.*

Above: Captain Edward H. Watson was found guilty of culpable inefficiency and negligence for his part in the wreck of the *Delphy* and six other ships under his command.

Below: Headline news around the country.

Watson and Hunter were eventually found guilty of culpable inefficiency and negligence. Blodgett was acquitted when it was determined he had not been the *Delphy's* navigator, as investigators had previously assumed. Roesch was found guilty of negligence, but all other defendants were acquitted.

Watson received a loss of 150 numbers on the list of captains, while Hunter lost 100 numbers on the list of lieutenant commanders. This meant that neither man would ever be eligible for promotion beyond their current rank.

Watson would go on to serve as assistant commandant of the Fourteenth Naval District at Pearl Harbor before retiring six years later in 1929. He died in 1942. Hunter served as navigator on the battleship *Nevada*, first lieutenant of the *Oklahoma*, and instructor at the Naval War College. He also retired in 1929. He died in 1948.

Blodgett was promoted to full lieutenant in 1926 and lieutenant commander in 1941. He continued on active duty until 1947, commanding naval ammunitions depots in Hawaii during and after World War II. He died in 1958.

William Calhoun retired in 1946 as a four-star admiral after forty-four years of service. During World War II he ran logistic support of the Pacific fleet and naval shore-based establishments in the entire Pacific area. He died in 1963.

Eugene Dooman spent much of his diplomatic career before World War II in Japan. His work was often characterized by an inability to convince his superiors to pay attention to his advice and expertise as relations with Japan deteriorated. This included a failed attempt to set up a meeting between the Japanese Prime Minister and the American President in the fall of 1941, during which Japan hoped to agree to concessions and withdrawal from China in order to avoid war with the United States. Dooman later helped draft the Potsdam Proclamation defining terms for the Japanese surrender in 1945. He died in 1969.

As for the seven wrecked ships, they were stripped by the Navy of sensitive and valuable equipment. Their hulks remained in the surf as a series of salvage contracts failed to be honored. They were something of a tourist attraction for many years, an embarrassing reminder to the Navy of one of its worst days. They were eventually blown up and dragged into the sea. To visit the site today (named on maps as Point Pedernales) you need permission to pass through Vandenberg Air Force Base. A weathered plaque is located on the bluffs above. In nearby Lompoc, at the entrance to the local Veterans Memorial Building, a propeller and propeller shaft from the *Delphy* commemorates the tragedy.

The seven ships that survived the disaster were decommissioned seven years later in 1930. Of those, all were sold for scrap with the exception of the USS *Thompson* (DD-305), which became a floating restaurant in the lower San Francisco Bay. In 1944, the *Thompson* returned to the Navy, but only as a practice target for bombing runs. Portions of the wreck remain visible above the waterline in San Francisco's south bay and are a common destination for kayakers. The stripped hulk of another Clemson-class destroyer, the USS *Corry* (DD-334) sits abandoned in the Napa River.

In another interesting footnote, the USS *McDermut* (DD-262)—the flagship of DesRon 12, which performed maneuvers with DesRon 11 on the morning of September 8—made a cameo appearance one year later in Buster Keaton's film *The Navigator*. The brief footage remains one of the best available looks at a Clemson-class destroyer in action.

As with the ships, the men who sailed on them that day are long gone. But their calmness, coolness, and heroism under pressure are not forgotten. In spite of the errors leading up to the disaster, their actions in response are regarded as exemplary. Some fifty officers and sailors were officially commended for their efforts that night in saving the lives of more than 700 of their comrades.

The name Emmett Haines does not appear in the historical record.

United States Navy

This plaque is dedicated to the memory of the 23 courageous sailors of U.S. Destroyer Squadron 11 who died in the service of their country when seven of their ships ran aground near Honda Point, California, on September 8, 1923.

★ ★ ★
USS DELPHY
CONWAY, James W., Fireman Third Class.
DALIDA, Bartolon, Cabin Cook.
PEARSON, James L., Fireman First Class.

★ ★ ★
USS YOUNG
BUCHANT, Ralph K., Chief Pharmacist.
DUNCAN, Edn, Seaman Second Class.
GRADY, Everett W., Fireman Second Class.
HARRISON, Brian C., Fireman First Class.
JONES, Enosh, Cabin Cook.
KIRK, Edward C., Fireman Third Class.
KIRK, Henry M., Fireman Third Class.
MARINE, James T., Seaman First Class.

MORRIS, Wade H., Fireman Third Class.
OVERSHINER, Gordon J., Fireman Third Class.
PEDDOCK, Clair A., Boatswain First Class.
RODGERS, Leo F., Fireman Third Class.
SALZER, Charles A., Coxswain.
SAWYER, Hugh W., Fireman Third Class.
SLIMAK, Joseph J., Fireman Third Class.
TAYLOR, Max L., Boatswain Second Class.
TORRES, Enrique, Cabin Steward.
VAN SCHAACK, Vern R., Fireman Third Class.
YOUNG, Main, Fireman First Class.
ZAKRZEWSKI, August, Fireman Second Class.

· Lompoc Valley Historical Society

Also by Michael Corbin Ray & Therese Vannier

The Long Way